Episcript from the Cadaverous Brethren of Purity

EPISCRIPT *from the* CADAVEROUS BRETHREN *of* PURITY

a novella

ARRESHY YOUNG

2025 © Arreshy Young
Episcript From The Cadaverous Brethren of Purity
ISBN: 979-8-218-56095-9
Learn more at https://cloak.wtf

CLOAK

خَريطة

CONTENTS

Monomer I: *Holograms* 03
Monomer II: *Autopsies* 19
Monomer III: *Mirrors* 69
Monomer IV: *Hallucinations* 81
Monomer V: *Vestigials* 93

Episcript from the Cadaverous Brethren of Purity

شِكْل

MONOMER I: HOLOGRAMS

> Eye, to which all order festers,
> all things here are out of joint.
> Science moves, but slowly, slowly,
> creeping on from point to point;
> — Locksley Hall

THE BLIND SPIDER

According to Humani Al-Wasiti who heard it from Ibn Qahir Al-Tustari, the ra'wi (echoer-adept) of Al-Jannabi the Damned, the Moth Circumambulating His Own Burning Carcass: "Al-Jannabi said in the year of his manumission from the corpse of his father: 'My father went into the cave against the advice of his subedar-ascendants. The cave was larger by far than the city-rooms of the Palace of Mansur. Inside he met a demented spider, whose knees were seven warhorses high, excavating each eye to depletion, its gore rivering and hithering and thithering between my father's toes. All the while the spider inclined towards him. He trembled, for its sockets whorled with hurricanes of cataclysmic time and may-or-maybe retinas and these congealed, without aid of miracles, into oracular tissue faster than the spider could blind itself. Suddenly, with a mighty blast the spider did what the *Vivisection Book* claims Gabriel did to the Messenger of Lies[1]—anointing my father with angelic saliva, digesting him down to the hip and infesting the surplus with its own despised and prognostic molecules.[2] Several weeks I grew, a fetus erupting from my father's virgin cadaver, for he had joined the jihad against the vile Caliphate while yet unmarried.'"

"'At last my head emerged, filled by Allah with pre-eternal memories of the delights of Paradise.'"

And Humani Al-Wasiti went on, disdaining my revulsion though I called on Allah to shrivel the testicles and tongue of the defiler. "And when the Mahdi fled behind the Veil of the Molecule, he adjured us to scan the Moon which is the face of Fatima, the mirror of Ali Ibn Talib's light, for portents of the end of time—the Theft of the Stone; the Ravaging of Baghdad; the Degradation of the Beast Muqtadirs; Le Grande Dérange and the Fall of the Caliphate; the Death of the Law of Necessity; the Unifying Annihilation of Brotherhood; the Rebirth of the Radiant. 'May these be a Guide to you until I awaken like the Seven Sleepers of Ephesus and break down the Gate to Paradise.'"

---

1. In the Kerkur manuscript (MS 2871 in the Hezerdja Patrimonial Archive) some orthodox scribbler retorts, in purple ink, "You Lie!"

2. Actually, the *Vivisection Book* only claims that Gabriel beheaded the Messenger and refurbished him with the head of a prophet.

By Allah, Lord of the Three Worlds, there is nothing false in this account in front or behind. I pass it down exactly as I have heard it.[3]

THE NINE DREAMS OF AL-KINDI

Wherein the old dreams serve each new dream as memory:

1. The dream of a man ichoring cell by cell through the roof of a hospital, coagulating in clouds, rewarding rain dancing cannibals.
2. The dream of leafless boys branching from a Gardener whose roots are hellfire.
3. The dream of mashing slave armies; hooves, heads and human grease conglomerate into a pupal pustule rasping through a single lung.
4. The dream of stomping mobs. A wine press but the grapes are the heads of Sufi saints. Al-Kindi's gloss: "Muslim veins and Christian gore?"
5. The dream of a gargantuan finger raised for the Shahada, the testimony to One God and His

---

3. In the Gurjan recension the collator inserts without citation, but likely plagiarizing off-brand Khurramdiniyya traditions, the following: "The spider's first two eyes were twisted helices, those of Father-Mother Adam-Eve. The third fluxed Muscular and Aqueous Fire. The fourth was the lapis lazuli eye of the Byzantine Griffin. The fifth and sixth were that of Turkic broodmares or stallions. The seventh was the snownight of the Skinless Panther. The eighth was scarred, the Eye of the Caliph of Handless Hells, where the untouchables weep, unable even to touch themselves."

Prophet. Two angels tear off the fingernail. It falls and splits the Caliphal continent. (Here the dream discards the dreamer). 88888 years, or the beard regrowth rate of Brahma, will pass before the shattered community of Consenters will rediscover each other exactly the same as they were right before that cataclysmic moment.

6. The dream of a glandular Bordello secreting ambergris and musk. Al-Kindi's gloss: "Alluding to the ascendant Queen-Mother and her origami odalisques, surveillance songbirds, borderless concubines and fissile eunuchs."

7. The dream of worlds which grow like mold on fresher worlds and qadis who colonize qadis they disagree with.

8. The dream of a city of free-floating Colons or Metabolisms. A few of these wear prosthetic skeletons and skin; their fellow citizens think of them as unsociable.

9. The dream of an apocalyptic dreamer justly executed for perjury.

THE WAY OF THE BURNING MOTH

Extreme ascetics of this cult light their hair on fire—their "hands" claim the hostile Bar Huthayl—to warm the beggars of Baghdad in winter. In their fortified ribat-monasteries they are said to manufacture altruists using organs recycled from generous martyrs. It is decrypted that God requires 872,298 human torches to illuminate the infinitesimal hair bridge over Hell. His beloved suicide saints are miffed God did not torch them sooner.[4]

THE SKINLESS PANTHER

We appeal, *aqida kalamiya*, to the testimony of words and huluul, the indissoluble union of a word and its thing.

We heard Bint Hafsa claim, in the year she poisoned Feraoun Yaqub the Pessimist, that she read the following unpublished scrap, written in color-coded qummi[5] inks and subtitled 'The Panther's Leprosy,' in the Hezerdja Patrimonial Archive a few days before a prudent copyist consigned it to an orthodox furnace: "We believe that Men are made of time, shedding seconds like skin cells and that our hallucinogenic world congeals from these garbage molecules. Only the Panther is real, our Eroding Messiah."

The scrap continues...

"Her flesh will waft and stick to our daughters, our fingers and mouths; to the verb and reverb of Shahada; to the knees we believe we rub raw, prostrating ourselves before a delusory Creator; to our coffee bean warehouses and plows, the library of Baghdad; the blurry Sufi vizier Ibn Al-Muslima, the Caspian Sea; to the beards of the infidel Outremer Sultans, the smallpox boils of afflicted

---

4. The human ulcer and heresiarch Bar Hudayj asserts that, prior to the torching of the 872,298th saint, no man, Muslim or infidel, ever walked the hair without falling.

5. Cacophonic cobweb cryptography used by the extremist Imamites to entrap invertebrate emanations and gnostic silhouettes.

Hulwan. She fattens—reifies, makes real—all the cadaverous holograms of this world."

It is Allah who Knows.

THE CLAW OF THE SKINLESS PANTHER

By the night when it enshrouds and the day when it is bright, and the male and the female, the shurta police informer Abu'l Husayn Ibn Da'ud Ibn Muqlah Al-Fasi told me that he showed the following report to the Emir of Emirs, but was demoted and reassigned to the frontier jihad:

"The Claw of the Skinless Panther marks an illegal guild for heretical artisans. Their usual front operation is a warraq book emporium where illuminators paint and disburse storyglass pandals and satirical ideograms, the standard subversive rubbish. This contraband only exists to conceal pellet worlds of perversion, and it was only after fruitless weeks of infiltration that we could open the Door of the Rectum and expose the foulness within."

"It would be useless to give more than a few stomach churning examples. Better if you stopped reading and with aqua regia and lime sanitize the sectarians before they can breed."

"In a warehouse world, the storerooms connected only by scoliotic sewers, we met a man torturing a vast Caliphal Nervous System made out of the black market vertebrae and nerve fibers of Mahdi impersonators and Sultanic-Satanic imposters."

"Beneath a dome of senile stars, the surviving devotees of that heretical Umayyad castle art slather the hemispheres with fresco-prostitutes resembling the wives of the Prophet which by witchcraft ceaselessly fuck the Rightly Guided Caliphs."

"In the musalla prayer-hall of a continental mosque, an architect busies himself rebuilding Gog and Magog, Sodom and Gomorrah."

"In a cage whose walls are dormant volcanoes, there flourish entire kingdoms of children who practice the Eight Fold Path—skinning, erosion, excision, incision, resection, contortion, constriction, lyes. The children call the charisms and inspirational insanity of saints 'reskinning the skinless panther,' i.e. restoring decay to imperishable holograms. They are surgeons of death in all its forms."

"I rely on Allah the Sane the Immobile."

THE SKIN OF THE SKINLESS PANTHER

As he works, the sculptor ruminates on the story told to him by his conscript fathers, how they destroyed their own life's work rather than deliver them to the veiled idol smashers who, obeying the Mihna-Edict of Yazid, had cheese grated their own faces off, faces being a blasphemy against a faceless Allah.

"I was apprentice to [the text here is corrupt] and one day I complained. 'Why do we even bother copying down these prophecies? They will be, or they won't be. Writing and wrestling, warning and warring, waning like the weary moon, changing nothing.'"

"The head scribe mimed as if to throw the question or the questioner into a trash heap. 'Redundancy of redundancies; the writing, the copying and the whining about copying and the mouth of the whiner, the questioning and answering—all were foreseen.'"

THE PIT OF EXTRA PRINCES

> A hand for the whoring
> A foot to the lame
> A face to the faceless
> A supplier of Brains
> > — Songs From The PIT,
> > Bint Marjane Sanjil

Everyone hates a kinslayer but polygamy produced more brothers and cousins than there were provinces to govern or infidels to slaughter. It was the custom of the antique Sassanians to bury extra princes in the PIT to await the day when they'd be useful, but the Caliphs well knew there was no point in "pickling womanish pricks," pasty and paltry for any job except "pubic tag-team partner" for the inexhaustible harem nymphs.

The men are boreholes through a fringe of flesh. Bad behavior is punished by hanging these flapping princes on gibbets in a windy garden. Good behavior is rewarded by a visit from unveiled headlight houris whose lipid rays the dark congeals into organs, spine, blood vessels.

Rewards vary at the discretion of the headlight houri on duty. Lungs for six death-bed breaths; a cathartic scream; teeth for paan-tobacco chewing; delusory lips for paan-tobacco spitting; throats for coffee searing; a satisfying cycle of constipation and diarrhea; severed sensile noses (the houris ransom, weekly, a hundred Christian hostages to pay their perfumist); an orgasmic aneurysm; a brain and contraband penis, no release permitted but a brief erection.

THE OCCULTED MAHDI

> Its nature is that nothing can be affirmed of it—not existence, not essence, not life—since it is That which transcends all these.
> — Plotinus

The Pure, The Trembler Before God, The Gateway to the Coming Era,[6] The Lion of Ali the Lion of God but never named, never alluded to without setting a death trap for informers and spies. His mind is a cryptogram; his action as free from motive or madness as the human genome. He is a Messiah adored by many sects, with as many faces and groins as there are believers. Some, including Abu Tahir Al-Jannabi, claim the Mahdi is Abu Tahir Al-Jannabi, though from time to time Al-Jannabi lets it be known that he has rejected his own Imamate and accepted Muhammad Ibn Isma'il as the Mahdi in order to soothe the prejudices of the run of the mill Qarmathian.

And the historian of the Qarmathians Al-Baqalani said to me that according to Da'ud Ibn Abu Mohammed of Ahwaz who heard it from Humani of Wasit who heard

---

6. Lavish gates are the symbols of sovereignty.

it from... (here we shorten the chain of witnesses)... a piece of oracular oratory which only Allah can judge as possible or impossible, that "I plucked at that cobweb of Arabic expelled by the Beast, and a voice like harp music admonished me thusly: 'I am the City of Knowledge, and also every citizen of that city and every drop of every thirsty well, and Ali is my Gate and Muhammad Ibn Isma'il is my fortress Wall.'"

"The Extreme Rejectors, whether Harithiyya, Mukhtariyya or Karbiyya, are so eager to occult their Imams—tucking them away in inaccessible mountain pockets or astral planes of unexistence—that sometimes they will affirm reports of the Mahdi's death, even as the Mahdi impolitely whines he is still alive. When this happens, a singularity becomes a dipygus, the original Mahdi suffers the ostracism of invisibility and becomes imaginary; *if* he leads, he leads posthumously and vicariously through the tangible Mahdi elected to succeed him. Sometimes the Caliphate expedites or confounds this process by murdering one or more Visible or Invisible Imams and seeding imposters throughout the rebel sects."

"His actuality is that of being a phantasm, the actuality of being a falsity. To take away his Falsity would be to force him to exist. To exist is to die; to die would damage his reputation and propagandize against his divinity."

[Here the chain of witnesses has been maliciously vandalized.]

It is unclear to which Imam, or Imam-pretender, the historian refers when he writes. "He had trained a monkey to feed him orange slices. That's how the Caliph's assassins got to him. He never thought to have the monkey's fingers poison tasted."

A more labyrinthine version of this plot is found only in Abu Mahmud Al-Misri, that someone paid one of the Mahdi's slaves to run into the room screaming that the orange slices were poisoned, "but really it was the theriac-antidote which the panicked Mahdi drank which had been poisoned."

QARMATHIANS

Qummi Glyph: The Spider Web.

"Qarmat" means the closeness of one thing with another, the anatomical alliteration of conjoined twins. In organization a utopian alliance between the Ornate Ones—mystic-fanatics, maphrian parasites—and the Jointed Brothers comprising serfs, "defiled" craftsmen, and Zanji ex-slaves,[7] referred to in encrypted letters as The Enraged Ones (Enragés).

More than one witness asserts that the Qarmathian Social Front arises from the recombinant gore of the

---

7. In this era the Illiyun sky-minders—nebbish orators, optimistic reformers and mass educators—are of no importance. Under the Buyid dynastic heretics, they will prefigure fellow travelers as human stucco/ornament.

Zanj slave rebellion, crushed in AH 269. In his 'Asrar Al-Batiniya,' Shaykh Al-Baqalani, a hostile Ash'arite witness, says that the Qarmathian Ornate Ones grafted gnostic and prognostic dogmas, Neoplatonic emanations, and jafr-kabbalah to the worker communes and social synod notions of the Zanj.

The Ornate Ones describe the cosmos as a spiral minaret of darkness illuminated by sparks—mundane plagues and the genocide of empires—and the Bloody Red Comets of their Mahdis and Imams.

The Qarmathians as a whole reject hereditary succession, preferring divine adoption, a model which may have inspired the Muslim and European trade guilds, and which alienates them from House-of-Ali-centric Imamite sects. A Qarmathian might say that "Muhammad has given more perfect evidence of God by his words than Ali by his silence." Most Qarmathians believe in a cosmic algorithm and in a soul equally cosmic. In place of counting fingers, the Qarmathians count the emptiness between each finger.

The five Qarmathian Tyrants are Sky, Nature, Law, the Caliphate and Necessity.

"The Sky, which makes day alternate with night; Nature, which gives desires and regrets; Law, which commands and forbids; the Caliphate, which humiliates and punishes; Necessity, which forces a man to do work even a dog despises."

Some orthodox theologians refer to the Jointed Brothers as "the tree whose roots are hellfire."

This is how Qarmathians describe Paradise: "Where perfumists sell peasant sweat to Harem Sultanas. Where plow and scythe enjoy their labor as much as any Jointed Brother, Caliphs buckle down as beasts of burden, Angels condescend to sow and harvest."

ABU TAHIR AL-JANNABI

Qummi Glyph: A headless demagogue.

Adamic father of the Qarmathian revolutionary utopia in Bahrayn. Their Muktaana or Supreme Servant-Atabeg. A brilliant strategist and organizer. Prior to his ascension the Qarmathians have all the viciousness of Maoist guerillas but none of Mao's infallible, self-correcting dogma. In mysticism the Qarmathian Ornate Ones boast of their incoherence. In its secular programme the Jointed Brothers are too dependent on half-starved Zanj refugiados or extremist Alid sects like the Khurramdiniyya and Alawiya pretenders, who can make common cause to raid a village or desecrate a mosque but lack long-run vision and the science behind mass supply and siegecraft.

According to one story Al-Jannabi is slain by a disillusioned Jointed Brother after he rejects his own Imamate and imprudently hails the pretender and secret Zoroastrian Abu'l Fadl Al-Isfahani as the Mahdi. Abu'l Fadl Al-Isfahani murders many prominent Qarmathians but is torn apart by his supporters after failing to resurrect Al-Jannabi's mother (who either faked her own death or committed suicide to discredit the usurper).

Carra De Vaux tell us that for years the partisans of Al-Jannabi's Occultation kept a saddled horse in front of their Immortal Imam's tomb.

ALLEGED QARMATHIAN ATROCITIES

The Hajj

At the age of seventeen, Al-Jannabi attacks the Hajj caravan and takes hundreds of pilgrims and several Caliphal family members hostage. On the march back to Bahrayn, many pilgrims die of thirst.

The Ravaging of Mecca

Besides stealing the Black Stone, the Qarmathians plug the sacred Zamzam well with Muslim corpses.

Ibn Zurqaan says it took three camels to steal the Black Stone, but only one camel was needed to carry the Stone back to Mecca. De Slane impiously remarks that the rescuers must have broken the Black Stone into three pieces. An impiety repeated by Ibrahim Ibn Abdallah.[8] "It looks as if the whole had been broken into as many pieces by a violent blow, and then united again."

The despondent Muslims respond so rapturously to the return of the Stone that the Supreme Atabeg Mu'nis Muzaffar and his successors, discerning good policy, redeem the Black Stone eighteen times in the following decades; they don't always bother to steal the original. Opportunistic vassal-dynasties take advantage of this

---

8. The original Hajj infiltrator and shaykh impersonator John Lewis Burckhardt.

proliferation of fake Stones to build rival Ka'abas and invent thousands of hadiths to establish the authenticity of their family meteorite.

THE BATTLE OF THE CANALS

Al-Jannabi defeats the mercenary army of Abi'l-Saj. He burns farms all along the Sawad and marches on Baghdad but Mu'nis Muzaffar and the hajib-chamberlain Nasr cut the bridges over the key Zubara Canal, leaving the Qarmathian vanguard stranded on the wrong side of the Euphrates. Al-Jannabi pays a fishermen a thousand dinars to ferry him across the river alone. He rallies his vanguard and routs the Abbasids. During the Qarmathian retreat, Al-Jannabi cuts Abi'l-Saj's throat when the Emir tries to escape.

The astronomer Hasan Ibn Abu'l Wathaab says of Sabur Ibn Al-Jannabi, the son of Al-Jannabi. "He was a comet in the system, but no man knew what he portended, for he died too young.[9] What he achieved or how many weeks or months he advanced us towards the Hour of Judgment is a secret kept hidden by the All-Knowing."

THE ZANJ

The World Breakers. Black slaves who rebelled in AH 255, slaughtering entire Abbasid armies before being crushed in AH 269. Some of the younger survivors later join the Qarmathians.

---

9. He was executed by his uncles after a failed putsch.

ZIYAD THE FATHERLESS

"The Prime Umayyad Mu'awiya uses the opportune rumor that Ziyad was his bastard brother to subvert the hero from his allegiance to the Prime Imam Ali Ibn Abi Talib, on him be peace. By the Two Lords of the Youth of Paradise, Husayn and Hasan, we attest that it was Ziyad who murdered the Prime Imam's son."

MONOMER II: AUTOPSIES

A slithering of testimonial DNA.

QURAYSH

But according to others the word means a sea-monster.
— Sir T.E. Colbrooke,
Royal Asiatic Journal

AHMED THE MOST PRAISED

According to Sir T.E. Colbrooke: "The name which belonged to The Messenger on Earth, that which he bore in Heaven, and the name by which the demons revile him."

THE JURIST AS-SHAFI'I

"When we speak about the virtues of Ali, we are called Rafidi by the ignorant, and when I speak about the virtues of Abu Bakr, then I am accused of being a Kharijite. I will always be called Rafidi and Kharijite because of the love of these two, till I am buried in sand, meaning till I die." Then he said, "People say that I have become a Rafidi. I say—not at all. Rafidth is not my creed. Does loving grapes make me a bootlegger? Does admiring an easily defensible citadel make me an idolater of barbicans and ramparts?"

FAKHR AD-DIN

Shafi'ite, redeemer of heretics, and author of the 'Book of Talismans.'

THE TRADITIONIST MALIK IBN ANAS

Author of Al-Muwatta or 'The Level Path.' One of the Big Four.

THE TRADITIONIST ABU HANIFA

The Porpentine Proctor of the Hanafite rite. Barred from offering legal opinions after lampooning a rival qadi (an abuse of ijtihad or freewheeling juristic censure), Abu Hanifa atones by playing dumbshow, refusing to hear or even *see* his daughter when she asks if swallowing blood from her own infected gums violates the fasting law.

HANBALITES

At this stage the populist school of jurisprudence. Dead set against the Mu'atazila and the putridity of kalaam speculative theology.

THE ZAHIRITES

An extinct juridical rite. Their chief, Ibn Dawud, pronounces the first fatwa against the Sufi saint Hallaj.

In the Encyclopedia of Islam one finds the following characteristic avowal: "The latter do not accept kiyaas except as a last resort; according to them, analogy is like carrion, to be eaten only when no other food is available."

ABU'L MUGHITH AL-HUSAYN IBN MANSUR AL-HALLAJ

A substitute suicide-saint or surrogate martyr. A woolcarder. His family supplies the *prostoy produkt* of the textile towns. Hallaj names his son Hamid, the same "ism" or personal name of his eventual executioner, the vizier Hamid Ibn Abbas. Later, Hamid Ibn Abbas will pluck Hamid Ibn Husayn's eye out, while taunting the son to heal himself, for Hamid Ibn Husayn had promised to heal the one-eyed secretary of Amir Mu'izz Al-Dawla, delivering a surrogate miracle on behalf of his father.

In his days of anonymity Hallaj asked. "Who will protect me from God?" When someone asked the jurist Ibn Surayj's opinion of Hallaj, he replied. "I abstain. He is a man whose true character is hidden from me and from himself." Hallaj aims to be Judas Iscariot and Jesus Christ combined in a single sacrificial animal.

Suhrawardi and Ghrazali will praise Hallaj many years later. Ghrazali sticks to his guns when interrogated; Suhrawardi recants, but later recants his recantation.

According to Miskawayh, Hallaj says at his trial. "My belief is Islam founded on the Sunna. You cannot flog nor shed my blood. I admit the preeminence of the four Imams of the rightly guided Caliph."

Ibn Umar signs the death order, countersigned by the ulema doctors of law. Abu Bishr Ibn Al-Haddad, the Sufi steward of the waqf endowment for the Al-Hanifiyya Ribat in Herat and anonymous blackmailer, says: "After 600 lashes, Hallaj asked the executioner to draw closer as he had words which to him would be worth the capture of Constantinople (revealed in hadith as a harbinger of the Day of Judgment).[10] The executioner refused and the thing was done around AH ▓▓▓▓ but God knows best which is the true date of his death."

They cut off his hands. As he awaits execution, Hallaj circumambulates his blood which clots into the Ka'ba of sacrificial love which tomorrow will harden into a Sarcophagus.

Hallaj spends twenty years trying to find the frontier jihad, which he knows only through the optimism

---

10. At least one surviving isnaad attests that at the 400th lash, Hallaj cried. "Now Constantinople is taken!" According to Louis Massignon this was "the cry of the jihad of sacrificial love."

of armies charging towards ever receding infidels and generational caravans of exhausted refugees fleeing in every futile direction. In the 21st year of his apostolic mission Hallaj stops in what he believes is Farghana or India and preaches to a pagan mountain town. Repelled by their idolatrous (Ajami?) miniatures and monstrous rites, Hallaj fails to recognize the townsmen as pristine Muslims obeying hadiths long erased by the orthodox.

Caliphal agents torture Dabbas, an early Hallajian, until he agrees to stalk the itinerant Hallaj, reporting back to the Caliphate from Khorasan to the borders of India. It is Dabbas as rat-catcher who guides the ratonnade which digs up the saint in the tomb of the prophet Daniel, where he'd been hidden by his brother-in-law, the Karnaba'i scion whose concrete or concocted "Qarmathian Connection" will be presented as evidence at the trial. Dabbas disappears shortly after; he reappears, in part, two years later in the Queen-Mother's Museum of Schismatic Heads, his ruptured throat sutured with minimal scarring.

The Dai-Summoner and deputy of Sahib Al-Zaman said:

"I came upon Hallaj grubbing in the same dust he ate. His disciples told me had refused all other food for fifteen days (every 16th day he would nibble a kohlrabi bulb, like a butcher fattening himself) and would not drink water until after the 'Isha night-prayer. After he had thus refreshed his voice, he declaimed to worms until dawn about the adoration of God for God which is the self-love of the Saint, of abolishing the Hajj, of the Substitute Meat of Saints which would feed the hungry and supplant the Pillar-Zakat of almsgiving.

May Allah forgive his slave. Four times I visited him. I was a young da'i then, gambling my soul for exultation/damnation stakes. Each visit, though I knew the innovations he proposed were insane—he, forging glib isnaads which seemed more coruscending chains of demon shaykhs than authoritative witnesses—I sank into the state of one who overindulges in opium, for such was his infernal-supernal mutation of dogma and diction that I believed he had *changed* reality with his guessing gutturals and predictive pants, drab divination and clairvoyant cant; scorning birds, he begged an augury from ants."

In 'The Projectionist' we read the following line. "The enraptured Hanbalites accidentally ripped apart a gauzy Hallaj after his death."

His enduring ephemera includes:
"The Primal met nothing but Itself in the Universe and said 'I am I.' Sorrowing, It cut Itself in half and from Its recombinant gore rose husband and wife."
"The union of the Transcendent with the Ascetic Soul, leading to absolute identity."
"I transfigure the soul through adversarial love, God against God. I against I."

"A saint mirrors divine light. A prophet radiates sight, implanting eyes into the blind."

"Acts done in faith supersede hollow rituals. In fiqh, even the Hajj may be replaced by works of love."

Of Abdals—the suicide-saints: "The substitution of the saint for Ishmael's lamb."

"The love that forbids the shedding of blood and the love that demands it."

The Hadith Al-Ikhlaas is the secret of hearts; the Hallajian isnaad.

To debabble his babbling communion with God, Hallaj breeds the twisted helices of Aristotelian logic and jargon, Imamite jafr-kabbalah, Qarmathian qummi cryptography and ecumenical fiqh. His chimerical creed unites all sects in paranoia. At different times, each believes Hallaj is an unreliable double agent. Confounded, the sects conspire to "cut their losses." Only Shibli and the Queen-Mother suspect that Hallaj's co-conspirator was Allah.

Hallaj lambastes the preachers of predestination. He compares them to the father who ties his son's hands behind his back, throws him into the ocean and then shouts "Don't get wet!"

Hallaj preaches the disappearance of means once the ends are achieved. His enemies, shocking no one, rely on the testimony of a fictional brass worker who reports that Hallaj claims for the saints the right to "annihilate the means," whether the ends are achieved or achievable, linking Hallaj once more to the hated Qarmathians. Compare this to Shibli's impudent divination. "If you say a word they will report it in paragraphs. If you keep silent they will repeat what you never said."

ABU BAKR AL-SHIBLI

"We know the flesh only through his bones, the bones he cloaks in putrid clothes," intones Bar Shibli of the man they flayed against the Weirding Creed of God, his skinless master-martyr Hallaj. According to the chain of transmission which begins with Karnaba'i, Shibli stole what remained of Hallaj from the Queen-Mother's Museum of Schismatic Heads and entrusted it to the Remnant hiding in Khorasan, and it is said the head will never rot. As for Shibli "he made a prayer mat from his master's flesh."

The Caliph sends robes of honor to Shibli. Shibli thanks the emissary, wipes his armpits and "dries the robe with the dust of the Khorasan Highway."

He plays the Peter role except he never denies Hallaj but feigns madness to repel those whose strength would demand such a denial. In 'The Passion of Al-Hallaj,' Louis Massignon has Shibli say. "My madness saved me, whereas his lucidity destroyed him." Shibli discovers early on that *consistent* lunatics could be congenial heretics.

Shibli's rosary has ninety-seven beads, less those two names of Allah he kept forgetting due to dementia.

Shibli flagellates his body while advertising the damage like a carnival barker. He salts his eyes to stay awake for days like the saint Sahl Al-Tustari. He practices or pretends to practice the Eight Fold Path (the qadis suspect him of Buddhism)—skinning, erosion, excision, incision, resection, contortion, constriction, lyes. He raves theologically; blasphemes allegorically; fakes epilepsy while drooling double entendres scatty enough to shock mainstream Sufis while delighting Abna Al-Dunya sophisticates who patronize and feed him as an outrageous pet.

IBN KHAFEEF

Key pro-Hallajian witness. Paid a famous visit to Hallaj in prison. It is he who relates that Shibli threw a rose at the crucified Hallaj. The ablution of thorns? A challenge? Or a farewell?

BAR HUSRI

The ra'wi of Shibli who vocalizes his master's words and polymerizes his corpse.

THE CALIPH MUQTADIR

> So may a sailor conquered by a storm;
> resign his art, sit idly in the ship, and give
> command to tempests.
>
> — Lucan, Pharsalia

Qummi Glyph: An empty cage.

They name the boy Al-Muqtadir bi-llah, a wish-begging meaning "the strength and mastery of Allah"; in short, a satire, though what Caliph ever lived up to those supernal names which they plagiarized from the Ninety-Nine Names of Allah? The Caliphal Court is called by detractors "The City of Sloth."

There is an illuminating episode early on where the vizier Abbas Ibn Hasan regrets appointing the young Muqtadir as his puppet. As Muqtadir and his new retinue sail the canal which leads to the Caliphal Palace, Abbas Ibn Hasan sends a message to Muqtadir to dock at the Vizierial Palace that he might pay homage, meaning to rectify, i.e. strangle the boy Caliph. Muqtadir is saved by Safi the Hurami who threatens to cut off the boatman's head if he docks.

Muqtadir's mood swings are as gruesome as the neonatal hands of bread thieves pinned to city walls and more than one vizier falls into the abyss produced by the Caliph's tectonic tantrums. Popularly known as a "mammary-muncher," Muqtadir is consistent only in obedience to the Queen-Mother Shaghab, although he sometimes perverts the spirit of Shaghab's maternal commandments to indulge a peccadillo or grudge.[11]

Muqtadir is so tormented by doubts as to the fitness of the Abbasid Brood—a bastard lineage spawned, by recombinant revolutionary law, from the coupling of orthodox martyrs, heretic Mu'atazila and infidel Turks—that when his father Mu'tadid prophesies that his son will wreck the Caliphate, Muqtadir feels grateful for the proof, indifferent to the insult.

Ibn 'Isa the Virtuous convenes a coterie of waxen Caliphs to train the boy Muqtadir in what Louis Massignon calls the "ways of sitting with reserve, alertness of mind, calmness in war, loftiness in bearing, impeccability in the cut of his clothes...exuding the air of dignified splendor."

He feels surreal in every molecule; his flaws obey accidental algorithms; his jumping genes transpose themselves towards extinction; his actions appear like emissaries from the ornamental tribes of impoverished continents.

---

[11]. Miskawayh's judgment that under Muqtadir "women and slaves became supreme in the Caliphate" underestimates the Queen-Mother's skill at political smoke & mirrors, a skill which multiplied her few hundreds of origami odalisques, surveillance songbirds and fissile eunuchs into an army of assassins and informers.

Of sex, we might repeat with Racine that "he'll rest his head on that heart he'll soon cut out."

"Parched little yearnlings suck at dry air. Today, Mother's breasts are rented. Tomorrow, Mother's breasts are leased." The Mammary Muncher giggles grimly, saving face by rewarding the poet as though he were satirizing some other prince.

> Driven by forces which allowed no choice
> of paths, he stood by the man who had
> saved him.
> — The Education of Henry Adams

Mu'nis Muzaffar reluctantly saves Muqtadir, age thirteen, from the conspiracy of Al Mu'tazz and kills Muqtadir years later in a putsch after the paranoid Caliph incites a hopeless civil war. The triumvirate which checks and balances the Queen-Mother consists of Mu'nis, the Hajib-Chamberlain Nasr and a mash of doomed viziers clogging the Cog of Fiscal Suffering.

His fiscal scribes play on Muqtadir's greed. The easiest way to raise funds is to fabricate charges against rich officials.

The lowest of the Basilidean Muqtadirs likes to swear that severest of Abbasid oaths that "should I act perfidiously, may my wives be divorced, my horses stolen, and all believers released from their allegiance vows." An oath which terrifies his officials because it often serves as elegy for one or more upcoming funerals.

Muqtadir owns two ancient rings. On his left finger there coils a two-headed snake which bites the bearer upon smelling poison. The inscription on Muqtadir's signet ring reads. "The World Is But A Golden Cage."

THE QUEEN-MOTHER SHAGHAB

Qummi Glyph: A manumitted helix.

The Queen-Mother. Last of the politicized Greek concubines. Models herself after Qabihah, the Greek concubine of Mutawakkil but puppifies her son Muqtadir more roughly than Qabihah ever did her lover.[12] The Queen-Mother hoards a massive treasury, taking her cut from all disbursements, not excluding the upkeep of Caliphal fiefs. Money equals influence with army subedars, Hashemite pensioners and stipend-shaykhs. As political operator, she excels her son but though she does contribute her share towards the campaign against the Qarmathian terror troops, she is as indifferent towards the serfs as Muqtadir. In contrast, she indulges a genuine piety when she defends mystics like Hallaj and funds waqf-endowments which transform the fortified ribats of the frontier jihad into sanctuaries for persecuted Sufi orders.

Rather than plot, as would be conventional, against Muqtadir's concubines, Shaghab keeps Muqtadir from discarding them when he gets bored. In return the harem

12. Like other medieval Muslim women, Shaghab/Qabihah subsists silently between the pages of the Arab chronographies like unspoken vowels or guttural stops which subvert, refute, endorse the text.

girls worship her—though a few ungrateful wretches secede to form minor harem republics—and serve as the Queen Mother's prosthetic eyes and claws, or teeth and tongue in the case of surveillance songbirds, against court parasites, orthodox jurists, atabegs and viziers, for Shaghab herself is trapped inside a living harem that grows fatter with every bootleg twitch of the Queen-Mother in the direction of the fallopian exit gate, shrinking only after a period of stillness worthy of nirvana, dormant only long enough for a bedchamber girl to escape and slake the Caliph's nightly lusts. Muqtadir would free his mother from this cage organism if he could, but his Nestorian sages cannot decipher even one abstruse letter of the Solomonic Seal guarding the harem's pituitary gland. Instead the Caliph entombs 88888 Echoer-Adepts who spend their wretched lives transmitting the Queen-Mother's reprimands to Muqtadir across the several city-rooms of the harem and echoing back his gratitude or tenderizing the rare resentful rebuttal. Despite the sick fantasies of Shi'a propagandists, it never occurs to the Caliph that incest, or even incest fantasies, might free the Queen-Mother.

> The young disease, that must subdue at length, grows with her growth and strengthens with her strength.
> — Alexander Pope

As the Queen-Mother ages, the living harem has a harder time dieting. The flabby alleyways and flaccid pleasure gardens shrink with all the futility of a decrepit body; at times the harem's senility results in fatality, as when it absentmindedly walls city-rooms off like inland islands or digests colonies of freedmen manumitted for the loyal service of their grandfathers; the date groves smear with leprosy and the rivers harden into lard.

The matron-muezzins release the call to prayer in words which the hurami guards can no more interpret than they could Pythagorean Greek; in response, a gluttering of weird coruscends from the Queen-Mother's Entrail Court.

The stewardess Umm Musa explains: "Once, after her weekly head shaving, the Queen-Mother confided that in the days of Aisha certain prayers were spoken in a language unutterable by male leaning tongues."

This stewardess is one of the Queen-Mother's key chess pieces, until she is arrested for an overambitious marriage. Shaghab likes to rescue prisoners from Muqtadir's dungeon and put them under Umm Musa's care, a favor they are obliged to repay should there ever be a need.

Of the Queen-Mother's origami odalisques, there exists only putrid fish-gossip—women able to derange, on the microcosmic scale, a minister's mannerisms and thus sabotage his chances of career advancement in the exacting etiquette-ecology of the court or, on the cosmic scale, to derange his destiny and sanity, as though deforming his astrological planets, with disastrous collateral damage for the Caliphate.

The lurid myths of "headlight houris" do not merit refutation.

BOWL-FACE FA'IQ

One of the Queen Mother's agents to the Outer World. The Caliphal Clown Abu'l Anbas Al-Saymari abuses Fa'iq when he says. "He was a man so fat that he required two necks and four legs to support a single head."

AS-SAFFAH

The First Abbasid Caliph. Saffah means "Surprising Shedder of Blood." According to Sir T.E. Colbrooke, Saffah might mean instead "slasher of waterskins," the desert variant of burning your ships behind you.

ABBASIDS

The revolutionary cadres who trace their lineage down from Abbas Ibn Abd Al-Muttalib, the paternal uncle of Mohammed. They cynically allow the powerful Abassiyya Shi'a cult to acclaim As-Saffah's father as the Mahdi, a claim withdrawn in favor of a prudent ambiguity after As-Saffah topples the Umayyads. Subsequent Abbasid Caliphs follow up by slaughtering their inconvenient supporters, leaving an intellectual void which the Mu'atazila will fill with a cosmology, theology and ecumenical scaffolding on which to build a broad religious coalition able to attract moderate Imamites and Nestorian skyminders alike without offending the orthodox Consenters or contravening vested hadith.

ABU MUSLIM

In the Majaan suburb of Marv the first black Abbasid robes were dyed. Here was born, perhaps, Abu Muslim, the forgotten hero of the Abbasid revolution.

ALI IBN 'ISA IBN DA'UD IBN AL-JARRAḤ

Qummi Glyph: A ragged prayer mat.

The Virtuous. Greatest of that long list of viziers who "play with the Caliphate like a gambler and loses," a reference to the later Hallajian vizier Ibn Al-Muslima, the orthodox shield against the Buyid dynastic heretics.

Abi Hisham attests that: "When asked to nominate a Caliph the assistant vizier Ali Ibn 'Isa replied. 'I shall nominate no one; only let God be feared and religion be considered.'" When the pretender Ibn Al-Mu'tazz bungles his putsch, Ibn 'Isa is nevertheless banished for his treasonous impartiality but pardoned by Mu'nis Muzaffar on the advice of the grand machinator Ibn Al-Furat.[13] In a very Abbasid twist, Mu'nis and Ibn 'Isa will swear a vendetta of convenience against Ibn Al-Furat.

Ibn 'Isa's biggest fault is his own equanimity; tolerant but ambivalent towards Sufi ecstatics like Hallaj, he cannot

---

13. It was said (here we mercifully suppress the chain of witnesses) that Ibn Al-Furat made a list of the conspirators, but whenever he came to the name "Ali Ibn 'Isa" his tremoring hand could only write gibberish. This he took as Allah probably meant it to be taken, a sign of celestial clemency.

see that religious frenzy is a peasant pressure valve for that rage so convenient to the Qarmathian Enraged Ones.

On hearing a slur against his master's character, Abu'l-Faraj Ibn Abi Hisham replied: "Ibn 'Isa was a man as punctual to meetings as the planets. He championed the Consenters, the Ahl Al-Sunna and had a deep sympathy for the fellah serf and Jewish thrall which the tax farmers extorted. He lived by the Prophet's dictum that 'an hour of justice in judgment is better than sixty years of worship.' In his house, poverty and obscurity were fêted guests."

Elsewhere Abu'l-Faraj adds. "I was with Ibn 'Isa in exile when he received the news of the fall of Ibn Al-Furat and a letter of recall, a letter which at first distressed Ibn 'Isa but all his friends and assistants advised him against a rash refusal. Despite this he delayed for several months and in the interim Abu Khaqani was appointed as vizier. Soon after, a second letter came from Mu'nis Muzaffar imploring Ibn 'Isa to rescue the Caliphate. The deficit had gotten so bad under Abu Khaqani that the Caliph had been forced to approve a tax on trees in Fars."

These, perhaps, excessive plaudits Sa'id Ibn Al-Dahhan amends. "After parting from the vizier, Ibn Al-Darir confided in me that many of the courtiers resented Ali Ibn 'Isa and he was swinging towards their opinion. Now this Ibn Al-Darir had done more than any other to secure my position in the Diwan of Ahwaz (I, the polluted spawn of an ointment maker!) so I felt I had to agree with his assessment, though it was difficult to reconcile the way Ibn Al-Darir undermined Ibn 'Isa's policies with my patron's admiration of the vizier's virtues. But for my own sake I soon learned that in the Court of the Caliph only public virtue was dangerous. A man's private piety, being politically sterile, could be applauded even by his eventual destroyers."

"And perhaps he really was a secret idolater, for he worshipped economy and probity second only to Allah. He put an end to patronage and the selling of fiefdoms, put the book to the hated tax farmers and their rapacious harvest measurement methodologies, fired fiscal scribes who padded their salaries by allotting stipends to dead or fictional believers. As a result the vizier suffered a vaudeville of near fatal accidents, which he had little choice but to ignore. These accidents become more frequent after Ibn 'Isa slashed the army budget and alienated the court parasites—Hashemite pensioners, hurami-domestics, Caliphal slap-takers, the Queen-Mother's fissile eunuchs reproducing without regard to the quarterly budget. He took a grim pleasure in parching this human swarm of their bloodsucking gifts. It was said that Ibn 'Isa faked the Caliph's signature, writing 'The Prince of the Youth of Paradise' in Caliphal gold ink and that Muqtadir allowed this out of instinctive awe."

"About this time, Ibn 'Isa exposed or exorcised a Qarmathian maphrian parasite by noting the angle at which the creature sharpened the nub of his pen. Shortly after Ibn 'Isa was warned that partisans of Ibn Al-Furat had convinced Muqtadir to reappoint that disgraced vizier, but Ibn 'Isa's fears were dispelled when an Alid pretender resembling exactly Ibn Al-Furat was killed by the shurta police. Allah only knows the import of this weird miracle, but when it emerged that the man was not Ibn Al-Furat, Ibn 'Isa offered to resign, despising intrigue as he did and fearing that his assistants would be tortured into making shameful confessions. Muqtadir insisted that Ibn 'Isa stay and praised him before the court and the Diwan of the Sawad as the Caliph's "Political Father." Even as he praised, the Caliph encouraged the rumor that Ibn 'Isa had supplied money to the Qarmathians, which the vizier denied, saying he had only thought to seduce key Qarmathian Brothers back to Islam. And it was true that Ibn 'Isa had employed Fakhr Ad-Din as evangelist to dithering Qarmathians, for in the past this jurist had much success redeeming apostates. But I testify only Allah can distinguish which was the seducer and which the seduced."

Alp-Tegin Al-Sarraad, subedar-superior under the Supreme Atabeg Mu'nis Muzaffar writes: "Atabeg Mu'nis, mindful of the universal crisis and the prophecy of Al-Mu'tadid (On Him Be Peace), kept Muqtadir loyal to Ibn 'Isa the Virtuous for as long as he could, playing on the Caliph's uneasiness, fed by perverse readings of astrology and hadith, about the religious legitimacy of the Abbasid Dynasty and subtly reminding Muqtadir of debts incurred, the Supreme Atabeg having saved the Caliph from many a putsch. But Muqtadir shook those around him like an earthquake, ruining and rubbling enemies and friends."

"At the same time, the Emir of Azerbaijan Abi'l-Saj, whom the Caliph privately despised, excused his precipitous aggression by claiming that Ibn 'Isa had authorized him to reconquer the invaluable province of Rayy. Ibn 'Isa maintained a canny silence, allowing Muqtadir's hostility to the Emir do its work, but when the vizier was forced to sacrifice the Sufi saint Hallaj as a gesture to an orthodox mentor, the eunuch-chamberlain Nasr added his voice to the slanderers and with Muqtadir this voice was too often decisive."

...[We omit here a reckless collage of dubious manuscripts and the copyist's anachronistic witnesses and impossible isnaad]...

"When Ibn Al-Furat fell prey to the plots of Hamid Ibn Abbas, Ibn 'Isa showed courtesy to his disgraced enemy. He moderated Hamid's cruelty during the customary torture and blackmail phase, and even helped to pay part of the fines beaten out of Ibn Al-Furat's son Muhassin. After the fall of Hamid Ibn Abbas, Ibn 'Isa was appointed to a 2nd vizierate. He took no vengeance against the intriguers and even joked that he was grateful for the vacation time, though Hamid Ibn Abbas had extorted such vast sums, that Ibn 'Isa had to waste much effort in erecting a Bureau of Confiscated Property to redistribute what Hamid had extorted. Though the vizier outlived even his brilliant benefactor Mu'nis Muzaffar for thirteen years, his subsequent rise and falls prove again that virtue, unless Allah upholds, cannot even reward itself."

[In Manuscript Kerkur Daad (ض) someone has sketched a Clockwork Cog of Fiscal Suffering about to be clogged by chunky smears of squabbling ex-viziers.]

IBN 'ISA'S CURIOSITY BOUDOIR

Behind a panel made of a chatty but delirious metal, Ibn 'Isa has mounted a beating heart which weakens with every Caliphal disaster. Blood flow is revenue and expenditure; myocardial scars stand for "friendly" embezzlement; tumors measure malignant disputation and subversive innovations.

Hanging from the panel itself is a homuncular org chart, gestating on the principles described in the famous treatise of Ar-Razi. The chart's HR hierarchy replicates like liver cells, eradicates like cirrhosis.

Among Ibn 'Isa's minor vizierial treasures: some forgotten predecessor has pickled the mercurial brain of the Persian polymath Mohammad Ibn Musa Al-Khwarizmi in the imperishable cerebral fluid of a comatose Jinn. The brain interprets universal events using an algorithmic blend of mathematical manias, fatalism, sentimentalism and sporadic logic, making seasonal adjustments and abjurations when it feels like it. The cabinet also contains a clay tablet which reminds Ibn 'Isa of that rejected hadith which claims that "Adam wrote on clay baked from the bodies of the Pre-Adamic Adams."

UMM RABI'A AL-HARSIA

Breeder-Mamasan of surveillance-songbirds. "Her voice, when it erupts, will drive her husband mad. Her operatic daughters will burst, in vitro, from her lovers' throats."

HAMID IBN ABBAS

Qummi Glyph: A hungry latrine.

"My father was Minister of Public Estates under Muqtadir. After the ascension of Hamid Ibn Abbas to the vizierate, Muqtadir said in my father's hearing that he did not think Ali Ibn 'Isa would accept demotion to the 2nd rank after holding the 1st. Hamid replied. 'Why should he not accept? A state secretary is like a tailor; at one time he stitches a coat worth a thousand dinars; at another time one that is worth ten dirhams; a sally which provoked mirth.'"

Umm Rabi'a Al-Harsia reported the following to the Queen-Mother based on the testimonial tune of Hamid's youngest wife, a loyal surveillance songbird: "Hamid's ignorance of a vizier's manifold duties was infamous. While Ali Ibn 'Isa ran the diwans, Hamid spent his time extorting money from the imprisoned Ibn Al-Furat whom he accused of embezzling from the Public Purse. Ibn Al-Furat's former assistants supplied fiscal records showing that all previous viziers had requisitioned and spent the same sums. By Aristotelian syllogism, Ibn Al-Furat replied, all viziers must be embezzlers, Hamid included. Enraged, Hamid pulled tufts from Furat's beard. These tufts disappeared but the folklore is that they have been used as relics of fiscal power by more than one Satanic banker."

Elsewhere this wife croons the following couplets:
Here is a vizier without a black robe
And there a black robe without a vizier.

"The second verse alludes to Abu'l-Hasan Ali Ibn 'Isa who ruled while Hamid bumbled, perversity circulating through the bumbler like blood."

Umm Rabi'a Al-Harsia, on the basis of her own observations, continued: "Daily his ambition decomposed, so that Hamid Ibn Abbas brazenly abandoned his duties and purchased the post of chief tax farmer in some province of the frontier jihad. The serfs he squeezed harder than ever, thinking to buy the Caliph's continued indulgence; this incited bread riots which swelled the ranks of the Qarmathian Jointed Brothers and produced a body count beyond my untutored arithmetic. When drunk, Hamid would blather his hope that the peasants would blame Ali Ibn 'Isa, who did all the real work of the diwans, but everyone knew that the two men were as elementally opposed as the two gods of the Manichean dualists."

Hamid is a rabid persecutor of Sufi saints.

In lonely ribats, founded in the name of the martyr Hallaj, some Sufi ascetics report hearing "the knocking of a ghost of former fearfulness, that vizier who beheaded himself with the blade that beheaded Ibn Mansur Hallaj."

A BLEND OF FACELESS FISCAL SCRIBES

Some of the fiscal scribes are burn victims. "You don't need a face to do arithmetic."

MULTIFARIOUS PARASITE COURTIERS

There's no career ladder here. The Caliphal Court is a pachinko of suave no-minders politely bumping their rivals into the torture PIT of indiscretion and blunder. The successful courtier has rubber scruples and avoids decisive, i.e. fatal, collisions.

ABU'L-HASAN ALI IBN AL-FURAT

Qummi Glyph: The Broken Staff of Sovereignty.

Abu'l Khuttaab Ibn Abu Dujayl said:
"In the year my father choked on a date stone or died of gangrene on campaign against the Byzantine Kafirs (but Allah alone can decipher my mother's evasive eulogy):
"When Muktafi's illness grew severe, the vizier Abbas Ibn Hassan pondered whom he should appoint as Caliph. His vice vizier Ibn Al-Furat belittled Ibn Al-Mu'tazz because he feared that Prince was too competent. Instead he put forward Muqtadir, a puppet prince who more than once would deliver Ibn Al-Furat to Caliphal torturers."
Ibn Abu Dujayl continued. "You may reprove me but for all his avarice and ambition, I attest that Ibn

Al-Furat was loyal to his minions. He punished an informer for giving a 'fake' tip and took great risks in warning the victim, Ibn Al-Furat's mawla-client Mohammed Ibn Dawud, ahead of his pending arrest. He was, besides, prudent in policy and clever in clemency and it was he who convinced Muqtadir to sink the rolls recording the members of Ibn Al-Mu'tazz's conspiracy into the Tigris. My maternal uncle paid Ibn Al-Furat a sincere, if circular, compliment when he alluded to the example of Musa Ibn Khalaf: 'Ibn Al-Furat's fidelity to his creatures exceeded even the famous fidelity of Musa Ibn Khalaf, who refused to sell out the vizier Hamid Ibn Abbas after Allah permitted that vizier's degradation. Enraged, Ibn Al-Furat's son Muhassin beat Ibn Khalaf to death, adding seventeen superfluous blows to the corpse. As Muhassin's thugs dragged the body out, Ibn Khalaf's ear caught on the door hinge and was wrenched off.'"

He continued. "I quote from a report I prepared for the Emir of Khuzestan: 'Deftly he grafted fresh flesh onto the putrid bones of the Caliphate. Ibn Al-Furat used extravagance to overawe the enemies of the Caliphate and to conciliate the Samanid and Syrian secessionists. His delicate dependency on Mu'atazila bridge-builders exposed him to the hostility of the qadis, but under his regime fatwa not fitna (word-legalities, not the butcher's knife) is the policy. Only against the Extremist-Exaggerators will he unsheathe his sword, though himself suspected of Mahdism and gnostic absurdities. Notable successes include the recovery of Fars and regaining the homage of Yusuf Ibn Abi'l-Saj, the gangster Emir of Azerbaijan. For these services Ibn Al-Furat earned twelve robes of honor,[14] a mark of high distinction but which doubled in the duplicitous reign of Muqtadir as the mark of Cain.'"

The hurami domestic and Master of the Curtain Mu'nis the Drooler[15] condemns him: "Ibn Al-Furat's fatal flaw was paternal piety and no one could doubt that his vices were like the sunrise which darkens the almoner's lamp. It was well known that his son Muhassin had a hold over him and though Ibn Al-Furat found his son distasteful, Allah had vouchsafed no other heirs to succor his old age. If Ibn Al-Furat could not deny his son's viciousness, neither could the vizier deny the vast sums Muhassin beat out of traitors to satisfy Muqtadir's or the Queen-Mother's poverty or greed. Ibn Al-Furat even allowed his son to break the arm of the Virtuous Vizier Ali Ibn 'Isa, an indulgence which Ibn Al-Furat was to bitterly regret for it alienated the Supreme Atabeg, annoyed already by the Fars Scandal where, with the

---

14. Edward Fitzgerald, in the appendix to his translation of 'Salaman and Absal,' notes: "In Atkinson's version of the Kitabi Kulsum Nanch, we find...that when a Woman wished to ascertain another's Love, she sent a Doll on a Tray...and judged how far her affection was reciprocated by the Doll's being returned to her drest in a Robe of Honour."

15. Not to be mistaken for the Supreme Atabeg Mu'nis Muzaffar, a confusion of names which will erase the redundant hurami domestic from existence when a Samanid bribe, disguised as the common trade goods of a Diraani perfumist, is delivered to the wrong Mu'nis.

Atabeg as broker, Ibn Al-Furat had refused to sell the fiefdom of Fars to the Atabeg's protégé Sukbara."

"As to why Ibn Al-Furat, for all his cunning and charm could not conciliate the Queen-Mother Shaghab who, with all the redundancy of the planets, poisoned Muqtadir's soul against him, the following excuse was offered, that 'one cannot flatter the deaf or intimidate the heartless or wound an enemy separated by vast deserts of indifference,' the last an allusion to the so-called city-rooms and desert-rooms and ocean-rooms of that organic harem in which all sane men disbelieve and even the Sufi madmen have never witnessed."

To celebrate Ibn Al-Furat's triumphant release from prison and 2nd vizierate, the Censor of the Public Purse buys so many wax candles that prices go up 60% and commissions caravans, descending 400 kilometers from the Zagros Mountain Range through modern Tawella, to deliver 40,000 pounds of snow to cool the guests' drinks.

The official chronicler of Ibn Al-Furat's 2nd vizierate rhapsodizes that "The Commander of the Faithful drew Ibn Al-Furat from his sheath, and the old sharpness of his blade returned." Though he muddies this chivalric image a bit when he adds that "in complacent moments, Ibn Al-Furat liked to mock his defeated rival Ali Abu Khaqani by screeching in esoteric orangutan and pounding his breast, as Abu Khaqani was in the habit of doing when swearing a vow."

—

Abu'l Qasim Ibn Zanji, who was later exposed as an indecisive double-agent (his accidental suicide leaves us in doubt as to which side he finally defected), reports that "in that year the Qarmathians ravaged Mecca and Ibn Al-Furat was betrayed by his protégé Ibn Muqlah whom he loved more than his own father. It seems that Ibn Muqlah was dismayed by Ibn Al-Furat's refusal to promote him to a post held by a mutual but indispensable enemy, a perplexity of power politics too intricate for the impatience or stupidity of the supplicant. To advance himself he concocted evidence that Ibn Al-Furat encouraged the revolt of the warlord-emir Abi'l-Saj, knowing all that was necessary was verisimilitude to satisfy the Caliph's credulity or boredom."

"Ibn Al-Furat saved himself from torture by regurgitating his shell deposits, but the new vizier Hamid Ibn Abbas, forgetting his vow, tortured more money out of Ibn Al-Furat's son Muhassin. Though the Queen-Mother hated Hamid Ibn Abbas even more than Ibn Al-Furat she did nothing to help Muhassin, offering condolences but hoping that the two viziers would destroy each other."

Abu'l Khuttaab Ibn Abu Dujayl narrates Ibn Al-Furat's 3rd vizierate and how Hamid Ibn Abbas was delivered, despite the most sacred oaths, into the hand of the vengeful Muhassin: "The first thing Ibn Al-Furat did after the Caliph imprisoned Hamid Ibn Abbas was to swear an oath to save Hamid's family from his son Muhassin as long as Hamid disgorged a huge ransom, but Muhassin played on Muqtadir's greed and the Caliph forced Ibn Al-Furat to deliver Hamid's entire household to be tortured. Muhassin, enraging himself with memories of the torture Hamid had previously inflicted, shattered Hamid's legs and sternum, denied him food and—Allah alone can confirm it—poisoned the starving vizier with rotten eggs.[16] This sloppiness, more than the final result, nauseated even Muqtadir, already annoyed that Ibn Al-Furat had advised the banishment of the ever victorious Atabeg Mu'nis only weeks before the Qarmathians had attacked the Hajj caravan and taken several members of the Caliphal household hostage."

About this time, so Abu Zubaab related to the Caliphal tutor Abu'l Husayn—though Abu Zubaab later inverted the meaning of this story under torture when repeating it to Abu Zafeer Ibn Sulayman Al-Nahrawani, a caravan guard turned inquisitor attached to the vizier Ibn Muqlah—"Allah decreed that a crazy man speaking an indecipherable Ajami dialect was slain in the Palace, having miraculously appeared in a room to which no one but the vizier had access. The rumor flew unimpeded that the man carried the following: a dagger etched with the genomic qummi glyph of the Qarmathian Supreme Atabeg Al-Jannabi; a loaf of moldy bread; a purse filled with more gold dinars than a palace guard could earn in a decade (this was reputedly stolen by one of the Khazar Turks who slew the intruder). No two accounts agree on the fourth and the fifth item. Qarmathian prisoners of

---

16. An operatic murder for a bugminder bruiser to concoct.

war were found to confess on behalf of the dead and implicate Ibn Al-Furat as an agent smuggling assassins into the palace. These confessions the Caliph publicly derided and inwardly believed."

According to a junior scribe assisting the detestable Shamalghani in the Diwan of the Sawad: "At that time a blackmailer threatened to expose me—though The All-Knowing attests to the guilt of my accuser—and for my immediate safety I paid on such and such a date a huge down payment, delaying until I could gather irrefutable evidence from my account books showing I had no hand in embezzling from the charity tax. It was in reviewing these records of my innocence that I came across encrypted payments made by Muhassin, in the name of his father, to my superior Shamalghani which seemed suspicious, though at the time I had not been privy to Shamalghani's insane claims to be a fusion of Man and Allah. It came about that Muhassin had begun to patronize this heresiarch, a patronage which strengthened the rumors of Ibn Al-Furat's 'Qarmathian Connection' which the gullible Baghdadi Mob took as hadith and liked to associate with every successful minister, though those who knew Muhassin knew the man was utterly ignorant of religious dogma, orthodox or heretical. He only wanted Shamalghani to act as go-between to a hired sword of Basrah that the Samanid Emir had accused of wallowing so deeply in the pigpen of infamy as to assassinate a Meccan Sharif. Muhassin wanted to hire this man to shut the mouths of all the fiscal scribes he had previously blackmailed and whose ransom money he had pocketed instead of depositing it in the treasury of Muqtadir (on him be peace). Because of this the Caliph could not pay the Turkish-Khazar cavalry who then rioted, burning several neighborhoods and a portion of the Dyer's Suuq. This riot alarmed Muqtadir, but it was only the temerity of Muhassin's association with Shamalghani which overcame the Caliph's reverence for Muhassin's money conjuring fists enough to abandon father and son to the mercy of the orthodox qadis. So it happened that by his perversity the son Muhassin doomed the father though Ibn Al-Furat deserves equal blame for fidelity to his venomous seed. For the schemes of created beings shrivel in sterility."

Abu'l Qasim Ibn Zanji reports that "Ibn Al-Furat, the night before his arrest, was heard to incant the verse. 'Prudent as he was, he knew not in the crisis whether to advance or retire.'"

The historian Miskawayh drops the curtain, saying "when summoned to the palace by Muqtadir shortly before his execution, Ibn Al-Furat enquired. 'In ceremonial dress or the durra'a?'[17] The Caliph replied with soothing words, ignoring Ibn Al-Furat's question but requesting that the vizier dismount when presenting himself for the morning briefing. The vizier heard in these words the infallible oracle of his own death. For the proudest prerogative usurped by the viziers in the early days of the Abbasids was to remain mounted when passing through the gates of the Caliphal Palace. After that there happened what Allah permitted to happen."

---

17. The everyday costume of the scribal class.

ABU'L HASAN MU'NIS AL-MUZAFFAR THE EUNUCH

Qummi Glyph: The Pre-Islamic sword Dhu'l Hayat, the "Master of Life" which impaled the fetal prophet Shuqayr Ibn Hunayn Ibn Al-Zanji Al-Athram in his mother's womb, incidentally discrediting Al-Athram's prophecy that he would be delivered stillborn.

The Victorious with whom Allah is well pleased. A Greek eunuch and Supreme Atabeg of the Caliphal army. Prototype of the Defenders of the Faith, who in the future will mostly be Turkic strongmen. Loyal to the point of "perverting the virtue of his virtue" as Ibn Khallikan puts it; his sense of honor, like feudal bushido, permits the occasional patriotic betrayal. Twice he saves Muqtadir from a putsch. Twice he deposes Muqtadir in a putsch and finally kills the Caliph after ignoring several assassination attempts which Muqtadir characteristically bungles. Mu'nis is not a genius. He saves more than one Caliph but cannot save the Caliphate, even with the help of the virtuous vizier Ali Ibn 'Isa.

Mu'nis flies from battlefield to battlefield putting down schismatic revolts. His opponents, for whom he feels no hatred, are Da'i Summoners sowing the semen of the prenatal Fatimid Caliphs, Al-Maariqun Deserters dithering between their rancor towards Ali and the murderers of Ali, Zanji slave rebels, Daylamite warmachs, the Qarmathian working class utopians and their parasite maphrians.

Only the Qarmathians defy his predestined victory. Their influence is a sphere whose center is everybody and whose circumference is nowhere. Even the Qarmathian parasite maphrians do not know how many fiscal scribes and subedar-captains they have infested. They mimic the host so exactly that often they stay buried forever, a muscle twitch the single proof that they ever existed (the maphrian casualty rate is kept secret, lest it sap revolutionary morale). The survivors may do countless heroic deeds on behalf of the Caliphate before erupting to open a single castle gate or murder some piddling minister. Even the Ornate Ones find paranoia prudent, for maphrians sometimes infest Qarmathians and other maphrians. As for Mu'nis, he is disturbed by dreams of enemy armies respiring in unison and the chests of trusted friends opening like coffins to reveal abortive grubs.[18]

It is to fight these no-minders that Mu'nis conscripts a vast army of slave-soldiers, Khazar and Caghri Turks predominating. Even more than their own slavery, the futility of fighting randomized ally-defectors drives the soldiers to mutiny. Mu'nis is forced to stage avengable atrocities and manufacture a schismatic army indoctrinated by readymade Mahdis, just so the Caliph's soldiers can have a comprehensible enemy to fight. These new schismatics necessitate the invention of a heretic dynasty whose apocryphal Imams will inspire the up and coming Fatimids; only the implausibility of too intricate

---

18. That he never suspects himself is proof that there are limits to even military paranoia.

a backstory, and a pious aversion to the symmetry demanded by his own Greek-Infidel heredity, keeps Mu'nis from adding a planet to round out his world-building.

Idle and eidolon armies fight each other with believable savagery. One of the several knockoff armies, otakus for authenticity, ravages Fars and enslaves several thousand men, women and children of Basra; later they dump their prisoners on some plagueland of the frontier jihad and tell them to found fortified colonies to ward off either the Ostikan secessionists of Armenia or Daylami raiders.

Cheering these holographic hostilities, Muqtadir lauds Supreme Atabeg Mu'nis as the Caliph's "Victorious Father" and bestows ever more lavish robes of honor, while poisoning his Atabeg's mawla-clients and subedar-descendants.

A prophecy attributed to the Caliph Al-Mu'tadid (or Al-Mutadid's astrologer) is that a great warrior, described as a Lion who saves the Caliphate from Tigers, will betray Muqtadir. The prophecy also foretells that the betrayer will appoint his own murderer as Caliph and so it happened, the puppet Al-Qahir executing his Greek puppet master in AH 321.

AL-SULI

Poet, grammarian, tutor of Radi (the "uterine brother" of Muqtadir's heir Harun), compiler of Qarmathian atrocities. Court Companion (nadim) of Muqtadir. Best chess player of his era; refutes, illustriously, the popular screeds against chess players, "that neurotic breed who never fast except when hungry [due to excessive chess playing]."

The two times Muqtadir beats his weakened nadim are both during Ramadan.

Dies in exile due to his antipathy towards Ali. A posthumous plagiarist.

NASR OR THE EUNUCH-CHAMBERLAIN OF TEARS

Qummi Glyph: A tarnished silver ring.

The Eunuch-Chamberlain (hajib) to Muqtadir. A butterfly collector and dilettante-militant who pupates into a competent subedar-descendant captain during the Qarmathian crisis. He dies of a fever during the Euphrates campaign against the Qarmathian leader Al-Jannabi.

Nasr controls access to Muqtadir and reads his confidential letters. At various times he flip-flops in his loyalty to Ibn Al-Furat, Ali Ibn 'Isa, Mu'nis Muzaffar, Hamid Ibn Abbas, though he never betrays his patron the Queen-Mother Shaghab, and treasures the saint Ibn Mansur Hallaj as erotically as an uncut lover would a perfumed letter from his inmate-concubine.

ABU TAYYIB AL-MUTANABBI

Ibn Khallikan, in his 'Deaths of Eminent Men and the Sons of the Epoch,' writes: "Ibn Uashiq mentions in that chapter of his Umda which treats of the good and harm done by poetry, that Abu Tayyib Al-Mutanabbi, on seeing himself vanquished, was taking to flight, when his slave addressed him in these terms: 'Let it never be said that you fled from combat; you, who are the author of this verse: The horse, the desert, the night they know me; sword and lance; paper[19] and pen!'"

"Upon this Al-Mutanabbi turned back and fought till he was slain."

Mutanabbi's rival ▓▓▓▓ [the name is missing in all manuscripts] derides this "spurious fable of a glorious end" with the following pseudo-Dantesque verses (which might have delighted Miguel Asin Palacios):

> He regrets his regret
> which laid brick
> to this Hell of
> Brave Deaths housing
> Cowards who repent
> With their last breath

He is born in Kufa but tents with Bedouin until he masters pure Arabic. Called The Ignorant, a compliment as his peers consider that he came within three forgivable flaws of the perfection achieved by the poets of the Pre-Islamic Time of Ignorance.

At thirteen he proclaims himself a god and leads the Bedouins in a holy war against the Abbasids. Mutanabbi claims he's the first to "prophesy through poetry." Despite the supernal splendor of his qasidas, the Abbasids crush Mutanabbi's jihad on behalf of Mutanabbi.

According to his ra'wi, the same echoer-adept who supplied Mutanabbi's epitaph to Ibn Uashiq: "In the year the Qarmathians plugged the sacred Zamzam

---

19. The Arabic word is qirtas or Egyptian papyrus.

well with Muslim corpses, my Master Abu Tayyib Al-Mutanabbi was taken hostage by them, for he had snuck into their camp in search of the Black Stone which the Jointed Brothers had stolen with much slaughter from the holy Ka'ba. My Master desired a visible charm of Godhood to regain the loyalty of his disillusioned followers and this Allah chose not to hinder. My Master kissed the Stone. The heat which fused my Master's lips together, as though he kissed a burning meteor, was not the seal of godhood he desired. The Jointed Brothers found him, writhing, and for four days he was unable even to curse his captors. During that time he prayed to Himself (and sidelong to Allah, when no one was listening) to restore his lost rhetoric. On the fifth day his lips were loosened with or without aid of miracles."

He continues. "To facilitate his release, my Master did his best to terrify the Qarmathians with miracles, causing his chains to rust and fall of, but they only laughed and reshackled him. They planned on selling him to some minor dynast who required a panegyrist to bedazzle his yokel mawla-vassals. My Master led them up a hill to show how abjectly the storm soaked everyone but himself. 'His hair is curlier than even the fatuous As-Shafi'i,' sneered a young Jointed Brother, and when my Master challenged the boy to a duel, the boy slung, with atheistic insolence, a goatskin water bag into my Master's face, slaking not the desert's thirst, i.e. spilling not a single drop. The Qarmathians mocked him and asked how it was possible that 'Allah, in fear of such a rival, had not Himself become an idolater?'"

The poet soon escapes from his purchaser. A long ronin period begins. Eventually he gains the attention of Sayf Ad-Dawla, the Hamdanid Emir of Aleppo, who makes Mutanabbi his chief panegyrist, one of the "Nine Gems of Hamdan," and subedar-ascendant over seventy mounted lances after noting Mutanabbi's bravery in battles where the testicles of lesser retainers "fled up their kidneys in fear." Mutanabbi takes no less than three arrows meant for the Emir. After each wound, Sayf Ad-Dawla compels Mutanabbi to write a qasida praising Mutanabbi as "the best sword Sayf Ad-Dawla ever pulled from his scabbard," which in literal translation might mean "the best sword the Sword of The Caliphate ever pulled from its scabbard." Despite this, the mercurial Emir routinely tires of the bohemianism of his panegyrist and, wary of the resentment of the court ("the poet's scatology made Shaykh Azaaz shudder in the loins of his father"), listens to malicious gossip and imprisons Mutanabbi in Al-Baaz, the Citadel of the Falcon, on four separate occasions. Each time the Emir repents and restores Mutanabbi to favor, but at last the poet exiles himself to Egypt where he flatters the manumitted slave ruler Kafur Al-Ikhshidi, attesting that "he who seeks the Sea despises the rivulets."

His Modest Reputation

Mutanabbi's intonation and pure dialect ignite the grammarians like forest fires; his recitations incite riots. After the poet's death, his echoer-adepts can hardly vocalize his qasidas without weeping. Matrons murder their husbands for the thrill and desolation of marrying and being divorced by Mutanabbi.

His Excellent Execrations

Mutanabbi composes a historic insult-qasida (other modes: kiss-ass-qasida, the lonely-hearts-qasida, funeral-qasida) which modern scholars refer to as 'Terror of the Paper Cut': "No one holds it against a man when, with a sword pressed against his throat, he wets his pants but what do we say of a controversialist who pisses for fear of paper cuts when a critic presses a book, or a refutation, against his throat?"

Mutanabbi mocks stingy emirs, calling them. "Solid souls imprisoned in opium smoke" and the "servile, second race of Heaven."

"'Happiness?' Mutanabbi replied to a blathering coquette. 'Happiness means for queens, fertility; for maidens, sterility; and for those who are near you, deafness.'"

He nicknamed the fiscal scribe (name redacted) "Jiraab Al-Dawlah" meaning "scrotum of the government."

His Understated Exaltations

He says expensive gifts have remodeled one patron into a Ka'ba of generosity.

He would say of a fat patron that if his mule stumbled it was because "to his learning, thick as a mountain, was added the Nile River's weight in graces."

And off the cuff Mutanabbi recited this poem in praise of the Hamdanid Lion after a raid on the Rumi Infidels:

He heard two fools whinge
About the fault in their stars
But what about Sayf Ad-Dawla
Who deranges Three Worlds?
The sabotaged stars
Whether Infernal, Supernal or Human;
Whine about the fault in their Sayf Ad-Dawla."

His Laudable Lamentations

Mutanabbi laments Bint Mirdasz, a girl who lisped like the lost houris of Iram. He eulogizes himself, slain by arrows feathered from her eyelashes.

Sick for the leprous beauty Bint Marjane, he builds an altar made from all the bracelets expelled from the Paradise of her wrists.

JARIR IBN ATEEYA AL-KHATFI AL-TAMEEMI

Mutanabbi composes blasphemous vedas and veneratiae in worship of this poet, for "twice as a child I saw the poet pass through the side door of the mosque; when that happened even the decrepit would pause mid prostration."

We read in the Royal Asiatic Journal, Volume the Eleventh, 1879, that Jarir's mother had a dream of a sentient rope strangling songbirds. She took this to mean that "I would give birth to a son who would compose poems so insulting they would murder, i.e. silence, his enemies."

MUSAYLIMAH

A cosmetic surgeon who supplies several face doubles for Caliphal pretenders.

SAJAH

Musaylimah's wife and second-rate soothsayer.

ABU'L FARAJ AL-GHAREEB

A senile shapeshifter. After a notorious career as a seducer-for-hire, sectarian assassin and instigator of tribal secessions, the increasing flaccidity of his disguises results in his identification and arrest. Presumably executed in AH 312.

BAR TAHIR

Celebrated epigrammatist. A man with eye callouses from prostrating so often and so low to the floor when praying.

THE TRANSLATOR IBN HUNAYN

He begins with the liturgical lambasting of his translation-fathers then grudgingly admits they shared one inseminating virtue, that of gestating the definitive translator.

YUSUF IBN ABI'L-SAJ

The rebel Emir of Azerbaijan whom the vizier Ibn Al-Furat appeases by means which repel the orthodox Consenters. A desperate Muqtadir lends his repentant vassal a Caliphal army to fight the Qarmathians who capture and kill the Emir when he tries to escape during the Battle of the Canals.

ABU JABIR ZAYD IBN HARUN AL-FASI

A petrimancer. When well paid, his human petrifacts insinuate imperishable organisms. At budget rates, his fossil magic changes his clients into cemeterial cells compressed into archival bone foam and museum muscle.

AL-TABARI

Buried alive when the roof of his house caves in under the weight of a rioting Hanbalite mob who find his juridical rulings unsatisfactory. Habitually insults the Umayyads as cuneiform Caliphs. Discrete enrollee of the School of Historical Astrology.

DAINALI

A simp who forges apocalyptic books in the style of the prophet Daniel, using a mummified Syriac dehydrated enough to fool even expert Nestorian antiquarians. For authenticity he stuffs paper and straw into his shoes to yellow the pages. Muqtadir is a favored client. The higher the Caliph bids, the more centuries Dainali adds to Muqtadir's Thousand Year and a Year Reign. As a side-gig for Imamite clients, he falsifies genealogies to prove Alid descent.

THE BORDERLESS CONCUBINE BINT ZALIZA

Who sells five minutes of interkidney cuddling for the combined annual salary of a Turkish cavalry regiment.

THE SECOND TEACHER AL-KINDI

His students attest that the philosopher Al-Kindi said, after recovering from a senility which struck and seceded from him as swiftly as a Daylami fly-biter, that "a long life proves increasingly that the past is only neverness and nothingness."

His infamous 'Eclipse of the Dynasty' is circulated privately among influential friends when the Censor of Public Morals confiscates the review copy. His 'Nine Dreams' he shares with no one but his favorite ra'wi. From infancy until he is sucked into his predestined whirlpool, Al-Kindi loves to wash with natron-soap.

FROM IBN KHALLIKAN'S LIFE OF ABU'L ALA AL-MA'ARRI

"I was a boy then, and I can picture him. I look into his eyes and remember how the one was horribly protruding and the other completely buried in its socket and could not be found."

ISFAHANI

Isfahani's stone dolls commemorate some forgotten act of savagery and are the only instance of Islamic sculpture. His masterwork is *The Water Carrier*, a camel with a woman's head cocooning a baby.

SLAP-TAKERS GUILD

A guild in Baghdad for professional clowns and jesters.

BAR HUTHAYL

"To console me, Bar Huthayl said. 'Be doubtful about the death of your son, acting as though he did not die; be uncertain about his reading your 'Book of Doubts;' deny that he recited it every day in the Dyer's Suuq aloud.'"

AL-ZINDIQ

A freethinker suspected of Manichaeism. In between orthodox prostrations, he thanks the light that gave us darkness and preaches that the blank which breathed before the World was whiter than the leper's whiteness.

MUHAMMAD IBN ZAKARIYYA AR-RAZI

Doctor and maker of plastic organs. Detractors accuse him of being a crafter of plastic surgeons.

Trained in the same school of suspicion as Ala Ma'arri and Descartes, Lucretius and Bar Huthayl, Ar-Razi hardly bothers to disbelieve the Quranic account of Creation. If he worships, his god is that Molecular Swirl which bodifies and modifies us and rips us to shreds at the scheduled hour.

His ra'wi attests. "His views angered the Samanid Emir. For my Master—while sipping comet wine made from grapes maturing in the year of the comet, so the Jewish vintners told us—was overheard to confide to a friend that 'God obeys Geometry.'"

The Emir's spies also record that "Ar-Razi—at his weekly meeting with eminent spec-theologians, Sabian scribes and Nestorian skyminders—summoned philosophy to leave Paradise in order to converse on earth." A fine of 500 silver dirhams was imposed, but the Emir withheld the 500 lashes on procuring the gift of an astrological treatise written by Ar-Razi's brother.

The grammarian Abu Qasim relates. "The Chinese scholar had traveled thousands of miles to be Ar-Razi's pupil. He learned Arabic in five months and copied all sixteen extant books of Galen using a shorthand script which he invented on the basis of philological principles none of our grammarians could comprehend."

One of Ar-Razi's slaves attests that the man was not a scholar but an ascetic: "As we performed the obligatory Isha-nightime prayer, we overheard the man chanting. 'I adore the Sun Chief of Sages who has delivered himself unto 33 perfect stillbirths and soon will achieve the 34th.' These macabre words disgusted some and frightened others but our Master told us to attend not to the ablutions of others but to cleanse that which polluted our own bodies. Later I heard that our Master had been accused of the following epigram, that 'Doctors are a suicidal species, but frugal in how they kill themselves,' but it is for Allah alone to judge the import of such gossip."

Ar-Razi's Materia Medica includes: "Fumigate small-pox pustules with dried rose leaves and licorice and do not pop these until they shrink to half the size of a peach stone," and "a Father is only the shaper, not the maker of his son. The sperm is the maker, or something hidden by the shell of the sperm."

Ar-Razi's celebrated caricature of a rival recalls the Lynd Ward engraving of a goofy doctor ejaculating medical bills.

IBN ABI-BAGHL

Failed candidate for the vizierate. Wrote a book refuting the Quran. Believes that only atheists enter Paradise, for "God admires the courage of those who stake everything on crooked dice."

ABU IBRAHIM AL-NAHWI IBN SANJIL IBN QURRA AL-BASRI

A defiler of lexicons. One of those who believe they can make men and Caliphs virtuous by rewriting dictionaries.

ABU'L ANBAS AL-SAYMARI THE CALIPHAL CLOWN

Adept at Ilm Al-Muaamma, the Science of Enigmas. His favorite trick is to flip a one-sided coin. His runner-up is to call the coin flip wrong.

His pratfalls beget bugminder schools of slapstick realism.

His fanboys call him the Mundane Magic Father; his cantrips bend the laws of physics until the laws, like unbroken branches, slap him senseless.

He derides the supine historical astrologers who splurge a thousand gold dinars to forecast the wholesale price of the average Baghdadi's excretions yesterday evening, too scared to exult in the wilting grape and roses of the moment, the only future that men exist in. "For after long miseries, wars and carnage, we fools, less foolish than the sages, have determined chance to be better than the choosing."

To exhibit his derision, he defecates on the history books of Al-Tabari while channeling Heraclitus—"history is flux and usually the bloody flux."

SAMANIDS

Become independent in the year AH 278. Thought leaders of the Ajami-Persian cultural revival. They rule Khorasan and Transoxiana, first as vassals to the decaying Caliphate then as respectful rivals.

مرآة

MONOMER III: MIRRORS

Between dawn prayer-prostrations Ali Ibn 'Isa would add flattering admonitions and zoological apothegms in Sameeya Shorthand to the ongoing 'Mirror for Caliphs.' After the night prayer Ibn 'Isa would brood over that other 'Mirror' written by viziers to instruct or sabotage their successors and never shown to Caliphs, a cagey delineation of dynastic dementia, the genius of Ja'far Ibn Yahya Barmaki depraving from simp to chimp to the ambitious amoeba Hamid Ibn Abbas, the vulture of foreboding tearing appetizers from Ibn' 'Isa's chest and never satiated.

Virtue has its dipygus, the parasite twin. If Allah did not will it, then perhaps Iblis? In any case the 'Mirrors' were leaked by impudent assistants or an opportunistic eunuch. Mutilated copies divided by mob mitosis, the more infamous enriched with Qarmathian propaganda and perversities so repulsive that they inspired one society wit to revive Alexander the Great's apocryphal bon mot. "The servility of the vizier has stolen the kingship."

Allah alone can differentiate the sands of the desert or which excerpt below is Perverse or Righteous.

ON PRUDENCE IN CELEBRATION

The best Caliphs seek out men of learning; the worst sages love to party with the Caliph.

ON INVOCATIONS

Only God rules without counselors. It is no idolatry to appoint ministers of superior talent or for the imam to mumble the name of the vizier in his Friday invocation.

ON SPIES

Shun the eye of the eagle. If the eagled-eyed must be employed, use them for one-off espionage missions of the highest importance then cage or kill them.

ON BUDGETS

It was said that the famous architect Abu Yaqut Al-Isfahani, "after due consultation with his munificent patron," rejected the Emir's idea of a panopticon combining espionage and the call to prayer in favor of a towering muezzin made entirely of eyes, ears and vocal cords."

Barring such miracles of frugality, a doubling of duties can lead to substantial cost savings. A muezzin should be spy *and* prayer-caller. In their idle hours accountants should assassinate redundant accountants. Retired lion tamers can be recycled as lion fodder. Lion cages can receive the runoff from our overflowing dungeons. The exclusive directive of each of your bodyguards should be to protect you against your other bodyguards.

ON INSULTS AND TACTICAL DEGRADATION

Master the tactical insult in order to lure suspected officials into a premature betrayal. Conversely, one must occasionally demote or even flog one's nadim-favorites in public to mollify your envious eunuch domestics.

THE CALIPHAL STAR

The Caliph must be as an "astrological constellation," a predestined disposition towards virtue for all Lesser Muslims. He must be supernal in the severity with which he chastises his children; the angle of his prayer-abasements; the way he blitzes and never flinches from infidel soldiers; the delicacy of his diplomatic etiquette; his prudent procreation; the way he lavishes the public purse on ministers of merit and disgraces venal mawla-clients; dines daintily and not rapaciously like Falak the World Serpent; in his liberality towards insolvent pilgrims.

ON MARTIAL EXERCISE

Polo is more than mastery of horse and mallet. The God-fearing Caliph allows himself to lose occasionally. The tyrant always scores the most goals.

ON SHAPESHIFTING

Bowl-Faced Fa'iq reports to the vizier Ali Ibn 'Isa that Muqtadir often skips his calligraphy lessons.

Ibn 'Isa's bold remonstrance is to leave a copy of 'Life, Breath and Languages' where the Caliph can find it: "Calligraphy is the art of shapeshifting its readers. A Caliph who cannot shape Arabic letters cannot shape Men to be useful or righteous."

ON THE ARABIC LANGUAGE

Never commit important orders to writing as what is written can be used against you later. Let your vizier take on the opprobrium of putting his signature to treaties and contracts. Were all Caliphs illiterate, their dynasties would endure for ten thousand years.

As a test, entrust ludicrous commands to untrustworthy Messengers. Always make a Plan Alif, Laam, Ghrayn, etc., disbursing these at random to different bands of mercenaries, to see which will betray your plans to the highest bidder. Obviously, an Atabeg with sufficient tactical agility is required to execute the real plan on short notice.

Manufacture diplomats, standard issue, who believe dictionary control and protocol can deter or delay cataclysms.

THE HOUSE OF TRANQUILITY

A Caliph must keep his word to Muslims and tax-paying People of the Book, but judicious treachery is sanctioned by God against kafir-infidels like the Qarmathians or the Sultans of Rum.

The hukuma-philosophers can drone on about treaties and Daar Al-Sulh, the queasy stasis between Jihad and Submission. For the Commander of the Faithful the only choice is between the House of Islam and the House of War.

AGAINST WINE

"If a sober prophet has little honor in his own country, a drunken one has still less." A ratl of nabidh date wine tonight presages tomorrow's putsch.

THE FLOWER OF KERKUR

And he said. "Of Kerkur—both. I was the thorn. He was the rose."

"Gardens were before gardeners, and but some few hours after the earth."

Read Al-Dinawari's Kitab Al-Nabaat, a scientific survey of desert flowers, for its pure Bedouin Arabic. Read it twice to adorn your soul with imperishable roses.

THE GIBBET

Review all routine evidence twice and extraordinary evidence four times. For there are always two men quivering on the scales of judgment when a criminal is tried. The qadi should make sure not to damn himself by passing false sentence. We could say the same for the executioner. For if he beheads an innocent man he has made it impossible for the qadi to repent of an evil decision and made himself a murderer.

THE GIBBET

As nothing is unjust that finds justification in a past or future history, remember this. He who nurtures, neuters, nixes the best historians is sinless.

Gluttony is a sin meriting hellfire unless the glutton is an ambitious and popular mawla-vassal or minister. In that case gluttony is a virtue which the Caliph should encourage, in the same way the Caliph Muktafi once gifted beautiful slave girls to derange the lecherous shaykhs of the Banu (redacted) and keep them from uniting against him.

ON SOOTHING DISGRUNTLED JURISTS

"The steersman of a storm-tossed ship is so intent on saving the ship that he forgets that men, not ships, are subject to drowning."

The way to tame a disgruntled qadi is to glut him with rewards or to cut your losses and assassinate him the moment you can dispense with his piety. Later, you can canonize them so that their sainthood might pacify the discontented and their "miracles" can continue to serve you after death.

ON DEPLOYING HOLY FIGHTERS AGAINST THE SCHISMATICS

Remember that patriotic fanatics share more in common with enemy fanatics than they do with your regular army. Sooner or later they will make common cause against you. Put the zealots in the vanguard that they might serve Allah's purpose and receive His recompense without risk.

ON SIGNS AND INTERPRETATION

"A mosquito diverts its flight by the omens of the sky, but Man dismisses disturbing signs."

ON OLD AGE AND CONCUBINES

> "Have you stamina enough for an old woman?" you ask me. "Yes, I have stamina for an old woman; but you are a corpse, not an old woman."
>
> — Martial

THE HUMAN ALGORITHM

It is not possible to prepare yourself against every threat. But it is possible to bribe or torture-train your enemies to be predictable.

THE UNDESIRED GRIEF

Ibn 'Isa chides Muqtadir for withdrawing from Caliphal business and observing arba'een, all forty days of grief for a dead concubine.

SELECTED FABLES

"Tell the Fable of the Eagle, soaring above the ambitious in supernal hermitude, affecting neither the World Below or the World Above the Moon, a nuisance to some, a menace to all, the futile and flighty visionary."Tell the Fable of the Bee, reliable and mindless, sacrificing himself for the hive, one step above the vegetable who at least is oblivious to its own sacrifice."Tell the Fable of the Dainty Date Palm which, if cultivated correctly, thrives and feeds hundreds but if neglected for even a week it withers in agony, the most capricious of trees."

ON HIRING POLICIES

"The finger is not asked to see; there is the eye for that; a finger has its own business—to be a finger."

THE BODY OF ISLAM

Al-Farabi—the Third Teacher, after Aristotle and Al-Kindi—tells us in his 'View of the Virtuous City':

"To every organ its grade and task and to every grade and task its effective organ."

"The Providence of a living organism implies its health; let it be gashed or otherwise wounded, and the Reason-Principle heals and sets the affected part back to rights."

"Provide ample funding for your inquisitor-surgeons. The organ which attacks the other organs of the Body of Consenters must be excised."

"What movement of atoms could compel one man to be a geometrician, set another studying horse-breeding or astronomy, lead a third to the philosophic life, another to eat the liver of her uncle at the Battle of Siffin?"

ON GRAVITATIONAL ODALISQUES

Ibn 'Isa advises Muqtadir to spend less time in his harem.

"When he perceives those shapes of grace that show in body, let him not pursue: he must know them for copies, vestiges, shadows, and hasten away towards what is real. For if anyone follow that which is like a beautiful shape playing in water—is there not a myth telling of such a dupe, how he sank into the depths of the current and was swept away to nothingness?"

THE CALIPH'S CALIPH

The Caliph's Caliph is Virtue. And so Ibn 'Isa presented virtuous reforms to Muqtadir whose passion for beginning these projects is matched only by his incompetence in finishing. As Tocqueville says (Gerald Bevan translation): "But such projects are not the province of advice; no one is equipped to accomplish such plans unless they are capable of conceiving them."

THE I CHING OR THE BOOK OF CHANGES

The Human Body is the Book of Changes.

On Advertising Adversities
  8 in the middle quadrant means;
  Gastrointestinal distress presides over illustrious disasters;
  Smooth diction turns defeat into serviceable acclamation;
  Dictionary control presages victory;

TALES FROM THE GOLDEN CAGE

"And he said to the little images he had made, little men that danced on a spindle and little beasts that stood about, and ships that sailed on tiny waters voyages of no import, he said, 'Ye are but toys, and I am a man, and I am weary of idleness and stillness and solitude.'"

"A Basilidean cage in cage of Caliphs. "And Muqtadir dithered, divided, dithered, divided, an odd mitosis debasing from demigod to doofus." The Core Cage has no entrance and no exit but an infinite plurality of skies. The Outermost Cage is starless.

Palping season. Most male orb weavers live to palp, six frenetic days to seduce or be eaten by the disdainful female spider.

In some pariah cages, booted from the Congeries of Cages, the Caliph Muqtadirs hatch and fuck for six hours before being cannibalized by their concubines.

Our boy Muqtadir worships a pantheon of 887 Deep Muqtadirs. Our boy believes "I am the worst." And no shittier Muqtadir steps forth to contradict him.

"From the cliff I saw the prince—so richly dressed his sash could ransom the entirety of our tribal hostages from the Rumi Infidels—insert the clavicle of Solomon into the lock of that Gate which had shrugged off siege engines and an elephant charge, the Gate which Al-Nadim calls the Gate of Gog and Magog."

"I saw the ruins of Muqtadir's Palace—but which Muqtadir?—of which nothing remained but the doorway and on that was written 'but solitude now is my only inhabitant; how desolate the house when the master has gone!'"

Putsch and counterputsch. One of 8888 Atabeg Mu'nis Muzaffars dethrones one of the surplus Muqtadirs. A factory fresh Caliph from a Deeper Cage leads an alliance of Muqtadirs or Muqtadir Impersonators to kill the Atabeg usurper. They ravage the Deep and Deeper Cages they pass through, triggering 8888 bread riots in the intervening Baghdads, supplying a causus belli for 88888 cascading civil wars whose battles will be attested by hadiths passed down by 888888 witness-Muqtadirs.

"To His Imperial Majesty. A Worm Reports A Diplomatic Triumph. To honor our embassy, the Caliph Muqtadir had his slaves unfurl a carpet woven from the flesh of the Pre-Muqtadir Muqtadirs. They moaned as we sashayed over their faces, our sandals scrubbing what appeared to be their drool in streaks across the ornamental weave of their entrails. Clearly they hungered, so primitive were these Shallow Muqtadirs that it was said they ate strange flesh that men died to look upon."

SHAHADA FROM THE HOUSE OF WAR

"We were surrounded, packed so tightly that our corpses propped each other up like Ushnan parade ground soldiers."

FOREIGN RELATIONS

The Rumi Emperor sends two envoys to Baghdad to negotiate a pause between forever wars. The vizier meets them at the Caliphal Palace, supplying a camel caravan for their journey through the Caliphal courts. Along the way they take notes (like all envoys they were also spies), seeing dead soldiers and birds of prey, the ruins of Ctesiphon and other defeated empires, a museum of schismatic heads, seas and babbling Babels, a dense country colonized by retired Palace guards, two adulterated moons, the living relics of lost Iram, and a zoo of burning Solomonic shaitans caged in glaciers. They cross the border of the Chamberlain's country-room and enter the Caliphal country-room where "it was said that the envoys camped seven times and rested before they reached the Caliph." The Caliph, son of the dead Caliph the envoys were sent to meet, greets them in full ceremonial dress—a burda over a rosewater scented caba-mantle and shirt of black washi-silk, the Sword of The Prophet and a fresh Quran hanging from his belt. The Caliph dismisses them with platitudes and the envoys maze their way through the Palace bowels, convulsing now with colonic civil wars and sectarian indigestion, the sinking and regurgitation of kingdoms. This time, having no wish to mislead the Rumi Emperor, the envoy-spies take no anachronistic notes. After many years, two archaeologists fresh from Rum (or what the antiquarian consensus had agreed to label "Rum") hail the envoys at the Palace Gates in esoteric dialects. Decrepit now and deaf, the envoys do not hear but wander into the dunes devouring the ruined suburbs of Karkh.

MONOMER IV: HALLUCINATIONS

GHULAT

The Exaggerators. Extremist Imamites. What follows is a smattering.

The Saba'iyya

Their founder averred that if seventy witnesses brought seventy pieces of Ali's brain to him, still he would not believe in the death of Ali.

The Khurramdiniyya

These heretics believe that Hell is the human body. Paradise is the absence of age and disease and a nervous system. The sinless remain pristine. The senile have sinned satanically.[20] These extravagant claims explain both the sect's unpopularity and orthodox complacency in suppressing them.

---

20. Here the offshoot Yusufiyya break with the mainstream, believing rather that Paradise *is* a supernal senility, a total disconnect from one's hellish body.

The Ma'mariyya

Their impresario Ibn Al-Labbaan repudiates the post-coital ablution. "It would be a crime to wash my ancestral sperm-Fathers off."

Some of the Exaggerator sects believe that the human body is a shelled sarcophagus. The shells from inner to outer are the Secret, the Heart, the Ruh, the Nafs, the Aql, the Cadaver. The Secret is the central cell wall, the occultation or citadel of the Self. The Ruh is beguiling light. The Aql is an intelligent darkness. The Nafs is the carnal soul; it only wants to eat whatever threatens it. The Cadaver is both puppet and puppet-master.

THE HERESIARCH SHAMALGHANI

"And I knew through ilham, my unutterable revelations to Self, inspired by My Voice, the Voice of Allah."

The most extreme of the Ghulat extremist Imamites. A heretic who taught huluul—the infestation of a man by God. During his short apostolic mission he converted key Shi'ite fiscal scribes, legal clerks, army Turks, and one or two viziers.

Having arrested Shamalghani's entire faction, the Caliph commands two of his worshippers to strike their god. The second worshipper, Ibn Abi Awn, raises a trembling hand but instead kisses Shamalghani's beard and implores his beneficence. The first worshipper strikes the second then knocks Shamalghani's teeth out, going so far as to spit on the prone immortal. The Caliph condemns all three. The unfaithful worshipper asks the executioner to first cut off his apostate hand and lips but the executioner replies "that it would be a waste of strength as your hand would only reattach itself to that body which soon will burn in Hell."

IMAMITES

"It was he, Al-Waqidi, who said that 'the birth of Ali, for whom be peace, was one of the miracles of the Prophet, may Allah grant him peace, as the rod was to Musa and the raising of the dead to 'Isa-Jesus.'"

The differing Imamite sects rank the first three Caliphs by most deserving or least deserving of hellfire.

Even the moderate Shi'a had split loyalties, serving the Abbasids who were children of the House of the Prophet but also protecting extremist Shi'a brethren if they claimed to obey the same Imams.

The archives of the Caliph Muktafi record moderate Imamite fiscal scribes decrying the hadiths supporting the Qarmathian utopian revolution but unwisely praising the integrity and courage of the relevant traditionists. In response, Muktafi executes a few scapegoats with no other benediction than this, that "men who have the impertinence to approve are no better than the infidels who oppose."

BY THE NAME OF THE MOTHER

"On the Day of Resurrection all the people will be summoned by the names of their mothers except our Shi'a.

The Shi'a will be summoned by the names of their fathers because of their good birth."

TO THE TEETH

Ali Ibn Abi Talib said. "I cut through his head so far that my sword reached his teeth." In 'Simplicius Simplicissimus,' that hideous picaresque of the German Holy War, a soldier and pig-herder reenact the scene,[21] as does King Mark of Cornwall in the French romance 'Tristram and Isoude,' who murders his own vassal for refusing to kill the king's son-in-law.

The Eternal Redundancy of war via Eternal Redentistry.

MU'ATAZILA

The Seceders. Their aqida-testimony is "We are the bridge between belief and skepticism."

The Mu'atazila profess to profess the doctrine of i'tizal or separation. They deny themselves the joys of judge, jury, executioner over Muslims who commit Satanic sins, freewheeling the implied Quranic injunction that "Allah shows mercy to those who secede from fake worshippers." Some historians put forward an older backstory, averring that the word i'tizal refers to a

---

21. Thomas Browne, relaying Pliny, says. "They grilled not children before their teeth appeared, as apprehending their bodies too tender a morsel for combustion." In the same way Grimmelshausen's Christ-Soldiers practiced butchery, not cookery.

sect that stood apart from the disputes between Ali and the Companions backed by the Prophet's wife Aisha.

They are instrumental in the Abbasid usurpation, the sacred-secular pillars of the Caliphate and a bridge to both Christian skyminders and the moderate Imamites but differ from these in that they believe anyone can become Imam who defends Reason, Faith, and the Sunna-habits of the Prophet. Some of the ulema think the Mu'atazila should be exterminated for their denial of an uncreated Koran and complacence regarding extremist Shi'a sects. Their bumbling battles with the Qarmathian revolutionaries don't do their reputation much good. The first cracks in the pillar appear when Al-Ash'ari breaks away in AH 300 and the Hanbalites riot. At last the Ahl Al-Hadith call in the Seljuqs to sweep the heterodox atheists from power.

THE CONCRETE MU'ATAZILA SCHOOLS.

The Basra School is prudently Orthodox. The Baghdad School enlists most of the Alid and Imamite sympathizers. Both schools consider that a manlike God is alright for the bugminder Mob, but they persecute any skyminder or man of letters who dares anthropomorphize God. They hold that any anthropomorphism found in the Quran is metaphor.

THE SPECULATIVE MU'ATAZILA SCHOOLS

The Gurjani School are data fanatics. The more they know, the less they resemble what they know. They can predict the past but can't predict what a man forewarned by oracular databases will dare to alter.

DOGMATIC DOUBTS OF PROMINENT MU'ATAZILA

"Allah never does Good, for that would imply some flaw within him that needs improvement and we can find no flaw in Allah."

"In knowing Himself Allah would become divided and would be Himself guilty of idolatry. Thus He does not know Himself nor does He love Himself."

Against the Jahmiyya sect, the Mu'atazila believe that evil and pain are accidents that have not been created by Allah; some pseudo-Mu'atazila philosophers dare to speculate that evil is invisible to Allah.

A BLASPHEMOUS ANIMAL ALLEGORY OF GOD.

The Mu'atazila like to recount the tale of a righteous klutz, a silk merchant based in "putrid" Bardha'a,[22] the "Baghdad" of Armenia whose native traders the merchant derided as "bringers of sand to the desert." One day this man trips over a cliff and is caught by a Hand descending from the Moon. The klutz gratefully worships the Hand and is instantly poop chuted to Hell. For God is the handless incel; He cannot touch or be touched; to anthropomorphize God is an unforgivable heresy; a true believer would have recognized the Hand as belonging to Satan.

---

22. Ruined, says Ibn Hawkal, by "evil rulers and lunatics."

WASIL IBN ATA

The Mu'atazila, their spiritual Father.

Known for his lisp, and his vendetta against the letter 'r.' An unbroken tradition attests that Ibn Ata once declaimed for five hours without once using the offending letter by making deft allusions, inventing words, and drawing from a fat database of synonyms. He showed the same genius in poetry, nicknaming, trash talking, Quranic exegesis.

SUFIS

The Ahl Al-Ghareeb—People of the Strange. Saints according to some; Aberrants or Frauds to others.

The qadis define two related "Sufi Problems." The first is the tranquilizing effect of mysticism; the mystic is numb to the terror of hellfire which alone deters bestial Man. The second problem is political. The mystic in an ecstasy of divine union neglects his duties to the Consenters—farming, fighting, paying taxes.

The moderate Sufis sniff at the Martyrs of Love as howlers for holograms and huffers after the Beloved Murshid, the Unmet Boy, beardless guides whose shining faces will reunite them with the divine.

A FORLORN SUFI

> He loiters upon the beach, an odd Andromeda
> no Argonaut will come to free.
>   — Proust, In Search of Lost Time

The murder of an abnormal youth has left the Sufi desolate. To the Proustian argument that there were no abnormals before the norm, the Qadis answer that the Law was prenatal with the Lawgiver. A word like 'before' is meaningless. "Deviance is simultaneous with the Law. The Baghdadi Mob has done no more than reconcile the Damned to his co-eternal home in hell."

JUNAYD

A disciple asked Junayd, "Who is he who knows?" Junayd answered, "He who knows your secrets though you keep silent."

A rickety bridge between the mystic madness of sainthood and the orthodox People of Hadith. Most Mu'atazila and the rational Sufis like Junayd are atomists who believe Allah allows atoms to clot into accidental human bodies. The irrational Sufi replies that Allah made every atom to lust after reunion with Allah and that atoms join together to better pursue that goal.

Contra to the canonical Junayd's reputation for sobriety, reliable hadith have the saint cry out. "If I say 'this heart is burned by passions,' you say: 'the fires of passion ennoble the heart.' And if I say 'I am not at fault,' you answer 'your existence is a fault to which no fault can be compared!'"

ASH'ARITES

The jurist Al-Tirmidhi encapsulates this sect's hostility towards philosophers and speculative theologians.

"When a supplicator decried the hadith that 'God descended to the heaven of the world,' as blaspheming and equating the World with Paradise, Al-Tirmidhi replied. 'The descent is intelligible; the manner how is unknown; the belief therein is obligatory; to ask what it all means is an innovation inviting hellfire.'"

The Ash'ari aqida-testimony is a doublekind gambit. Mimic their enemies' dialectic until even Allah cannot tell the difference. Intellectually redundant, supplanted by synonyms, morally and emotionally inferior, both philosophers like Al-Farabi and the philosophically tainted Mu'atazila can now be digested by their parasitic twin.

ALI IBN ISMA'IL IBN ISHAQ AL-ASH'ARI

"This occurred in the great mosque of Basrah, on a Friday. Al-Ash'ari was sitting in the chair from which he taught when he cried out as loud as he could: 'You know who I am! I used to hold that the Q'uran was created, that the eyes of men shall not see God, and that we ourselves are the authors of our evil deeds. These are Mu'atazila doctrines. Now, I have returned to the truth.'"

HARITH AL-MUHASIBI

The Spirit Father of the Ash'ari sect as Al-Ash'ari is their Flesh Father. Author of the Ri'aya, a total manual of the inner life. The Hanbalites revile him because he ranks religious works by their moral worth instead of by the reliability of their chains of transmission. A theologian who weaponizes Reason against Reason. Junayd's master in mysticism and the only man who ever tempted Ghrazali towards idolatry.

THE JOKE UNHEARD

The occasionalist Ibn Ishaq Al-Ash'ari said. "The theory that Allah is able to boil the waters in which the covetous drown forever but cannot, lacking oil, set that same water on fire belongs to a book of laughable proverbs. It does not deserve to be refuted."

ALAWIYA

Pretenders to the Caliphate, they claim to be descendants of the Prophet's daughter Fatima.

SECT OF THE BLIND SPIDER

The Anbari Qarmathians are dominated by an Alawiya offshoot sect who continue to serve the insane spider rather than the Mahdi which the spider was created to gestate.

DAHRI

Specifically those who deny the universe has a beginning in time. More generally, an atheist or materialist.

SABIANS

The Men of Harran, or Sabians, practice a gendered taqiyya, obliging boys to be Muslim but girls to revere their ancient paganism. They believe angels or demiurges cause all change whether this be plague progression, the ripening of dates and olives, domestic tantrums, food poisoning, star orbits, earthquakes, the fall of empires, etc.

THE HEAD OF MERCURY

The oracular Head of Mercury was torn off a man the Sabian douarmen claim resembled the god Mercury. These Adherents of the Head immersed the hemigod in oil and borax until his joints loosened.

THE BORDELLO OF FIRE

By Allah of the Three Worlds, you're cordially invited to Bordello of Fire Ayn (ع), Golden Cage #379. A place where sophisticates are mummified in fire; they swaddle their children not to smother the flames but to plaster the pupating fire into their nurturing pores. Come melt into gyrating lava that chars! Coagulate at will, melt, clot, char! Some of our guests prefer to marinate in their own grease or to braise in blood and boiling seminal fluid. We have torments to doppel every conceivable pleasure! A subscription plan for every budget! By Allah the Opener of Cages and the Looser of Bonds, all subscribers are free to cancel whenever.

أثري

MONOMER V: VESTIGIALS

SLANDERS OF OLD BAGHDAD

The jurists say that the Sufis "always drink of the cup of delusion even if the cup be not wine but water."

The Friend of Unclean Pleasures slurs. "A few of the Strange Ones dared to follow right, not fate. But how few!"

Abu Bakr Mohammed Ibn Zayd says that the spec-theologian Yusuf Ibn Bajjah was so thin that he tied lead to the bottom of his sandals so the wind would not blow him over a cliff. Ibn Al-Nadim claims this slander was originally directed at Hunayn Ibn Ishaq who, "when he left the House of Wisdom, carried stacks of Greek manuscripts to anchor himself against a strong Baghdadi breeze."

And the shaykh declaimed or defamed.
"One of the on-demand Hallajian tricks was to inflate himself to the size of a mosque, making use of loose clothing and hidden vents. He claimed twenty believers could perform their prayer-prostrations inside his body without stress."

Another time I saw Hallaj summon an apple from Paradise, but it had a worm in it which Hallaj excused by saying that the apple had to be worm ridden as he had forced it out of the imperishable and into our perishable world.

But the trick which exasperated us beyond endurance was when he would pluck a fresh saltwater fish from his sash and an Indian monji cabbage from a "garden" growing beneath his turban in order to feed gullible disciples. Sneaking into his house one night, my son uncovered a hidden courtyard wherein was a pond and a vegetable bed. Later, accompanied by the Censor of Public Morals, I broke into this court of lies, but found only a pile of rocks like the cairns of Barawa pagans."

"...and that trouble maker Hallaj Ibn Mansur, with an audacity worthy of Satan, resurrected both parrots—the first parrot must have been annoyed at the resurrection of the rival which had just pecked him to death—in order to preserve the ancient tongue of the Himyarites or Iram or whatever extinct voice the saint's deranged mind imagined these geriatric birds were capable of mimicking..."

Al-Buzanajirdi asks. "Or is it Shibli who robs the Queen-Mother's museum of Schismatic Heads, sutures Hallaj to his neck, severed hands to his stumps, all the above to his trunk—drawn and quartered and thrown into the Tigris River but fished out by his remnant disciples?"

"The Imposter Enoch accused the Emir of Azerbaijan of worshipping with the Muslims on Friday, the Jews on Saturday and drinking wine with Sunday Christians."

SLANDERS OF NEW BAGHDAD

Sa'di, in his 'Lives of the Gluttons,' says. "If the Sun in place of bread did his table grace, no one would ever see the light again."

"For three months Abu Qahtaba Ibn Shabib had tormented his wife by refusing to have sex with her, though he denied that he desired divorce. One month more and the chastity Laws would enforce what he did not desire, unless his wife invoked mukhlif and took an interim lover."

"The poet of decadence Ibn Yahya Al-Juwaini has dyed his hair red because some toyminder told him that Munkar and Nakir—the angelic lawyers who cross-examine the dead—recoil from red-haired corpses in disgust."

"Twice the funeral pyre rejected the fuel and refused to incinerate the Consenters. The puzzled executioner of the Buyid Emirs set his victims to one side in order to inspect the wood, which even for that season was extra dry. He tripped and what happened was what Allah permitted to happen. For instantly a pillar of fire shot up to Paradise."

THE RESURRECTION OF THE WORD

"The book opens. If orators arise from these pages, my hand suffices as a pulpit for their speeches. If witnesses arise to accuse me I am condemned, if to absolve me, from that moment I am a free man."

THE BOOK OF INNOCUOUS PLAGIARISMS

"Many times I have happened: lifted out of the body into myself; becoming external to all other things and self-centered; beholding a marvelous beauty."

"All admired the Moth Brother's audacity as he voluntarily imitated the descent of Jesus into Hell."

"Hence every action has magic as its source, and the entire life of the practical man is a bewitchment but no man self-gathered falls to a spell."

"Man is the universal hieroglyph but what supernal Hand wears the decoder ring?"

THE BOOK OF PERILOUS PLAGIARISMS

"The intelligent abattoir which seeped from between the pages of Ibn Jabr's Grimoire and onto my library shelves has no discernible motive. It commands us. We have no incentive to obey. We feel no compulsion. Yet it is as if our desires, and sometimes our memories, change retroactively, to justify and impassion our inevitable actions, but of course such speculation is self-defeating by design, like the incitements of those accursed Ghulat Exaggerators who contend that the most vile and lowly of their pantheon of 888 deepfake Allahs has made dementia the congenital state of mankind."

The visitor to the great garden of Sanabadh will find, at the ninth canonical hour, two identical tombs and a waffling crowd of mourners. Whether Ar-Rashid's son Ma'mun poisoned the 8th Imam Ali Ar-Rida' or whether the Imam's death was fortuitous is irrelevant. What happened was this. As a sop to both sects, the Caliph Ma'mun buried the Imam with great reverence in a tomb resembling exactly his father's—down to the identical wear and tear he employs 800 slaves to maintain—so that to this day Shi'a pilgrims are not sure which tomb to venerate and which to deface.

ILLUSTRIOUS ANECDOTES

Al-Hirmazi told the following. "When a city woman was asked, 'By what do you recognize the dawn?' She said. 'By the coldness of the jewelry against my skin.' When a village woman was asked, she said. 'By the bursting forth of flowers.' When a barbarous woman was asked, she said. 'Dawn is when coffee best loosens my bowels.'"

An anecdote about imprudent advisers.
"An astrologer predicted that the Caliph Harun Ar-Rashid would die within a year. Depressed, the Caliph related the prediction to his vizier Ja'far Ibn Yahya Barmaki. Ja'far asked the astrologer how long the astrologer himself had to live. The vizier then advised Ar-Rashid to kill the astrologer to prove both predictions wrong."

The Poet Abu Nuwas exhorts. "Say to the trusty servant of God, the offspring of princes and able rulers. When you wish to make a traitor lose his head, slay him not with the sword, but marry him to Abbasah!"

Here the poet alludes to the Caliph Ar-Rashid who cunningly arranged a sham marriage between Ja'far and his sister Abbasah, and killed the vizier when he unwittingly got Abbasah pregnant. A fragment published in the Royal Asiatic Journal posits a more whimsical alternative, stating that Ar-Rashid desired to see whether Ja'far or his sister was the better chess player. It being a scandal under Islamic sex-law for the unmarried to meet in private, the Caliph presented the signed marriage certificate to the astonished couple.

When the Messenger was amending the Treaty of Hudaybiyya, he said to Ali. "Then put my hand upon it." And the Apostle of the Apostle of God put his own palm print to the document so as not to embarrass his cousin. This shows that The Messenger (Allah's Peace be on him) was illiterate.

VERIFIED VENTRILOQUISMS

> Augustus, Lepidus, and Antony were popular demagogues who agreed together to fleece the flock between them, until the most cunning of the three destroyed the other two, fleeced the sheep alone, and transmitted the shears to a line of tyrants.
> — John Adams

We revile and refute all "evidence" provided by orthodox lunatics of those supposed declamations where the Occulted Mahdi admits he suffers from Harlequin Disease.

THE FOUR ROSES

"The white rose was created from the sweat of the Prophet on the night of the nocturnal ascension, the red rose from the sweat of Gabriel, the yellow rose from the Prophet's winged steed Al-Buraaq, the green rose from the coagulating blood of the saint Hallaj."

Ghrazali assures us that every time we pray, a new angelic lawyer is born to plead our case to Allah.

WITNESSES (SHUHUUD)

> Though we pass our lives in investigation, all we can collect may be reduced to this; "it is said or they say."
>
> — Fakhr Ad-Din

> A relation made by Al-Shafi'i on the authority of Malik, and by him on the authority of Nafi', and by him on the authority of Ibn 'Umar, such a series is really the golden chain; so exalted is the merit of each of these narrators.
> — Ibn Khallikan

Ibn Ishaq Al-Nadim: Absolutely reliable.

Humani of Wasit: A fallacious form of feces.

Muhassin: Rejected. Son of the vizier Ibn Al-Furat.

Abi'l-Farak Ibn Hisham: Reliable.

Isma'il Ibn Zanji: Unreliable. "As treacherous as a Khorasani (cut) coin."

Abu'l-Naj Ibn Suhrawardi: Reliable. Descendant of the Rightly Guided Caliph Abu Bakr.

Abu'l Qasim: Unreliable.

Shamalghani: Demented.

Ibn Surayj[23]**:** Reliable in youth; unreliable afterwards.

Abu'l-Faraj Ibn Abi Hisham: Reliability scales with the size of the kickback.

Abu'l Qasim Ibn Zanji: Reliable for months at a time. An indecisive double agent.

---

23. The story is that when Ibn Surayj heard about the death of Ibn Dawud, he threw away the leaves of his study-book and became an opium addict, saying "the man is dead who was the motive to study, for I desired to debate him, not to defeat him but to hold my own."

AL-BAQALANI: Reliable. Historian of the Qarmathians.

ABU DABBAS: Rejected. Early Hallajian turncoat.

KARNABA'I: Posthumous ra'wi and brother-in-law to Ibn Mansur Hallaj. Two isnaads cited by the biographer Ibn Khallikan.

HAMID IBN ABBAS: Unreliable. Chief persecutor of Hallaj.

HAMID IBN HALLAJ: Doubtful. Son and hagiographer of Hallaj Ibn Mansur.

AL-SULI: Reliable. Court nadim of Muqtadir.

BAR HUTHAYL: Feeble.

IBN ZURQAAN: Feeble. An ex-Zanji slave and subedar-ascendant commanding Qarmathian plunder battalions in the Ahwaz.

UMM RABI'A AL-HARSIA: Reliable. Breeder-Mama-san of surveillance-songbirds.

IBN KHAFEEF: Doubtful. Sole sympathetic witness to the despairing prayer of Hallaj the night before the saint's execution.

Abu Zubaab: Demented. The Father of Flies, a sarcasm meaning "Kinslayer," alluding to the way his bad breath knocks flies out of the sky.

Abu Zafeer: Unreliable. The Father of Misfortune. Also a pet name for the goose.

Abu'l Husayn: Reliable. Muqtadir's tutor.

PLACE NAMES

Khorasan: Famous for its flax paper.

Kufah: Moqsuitoville, as opposed to Baghdad.

Wasit: A hub for lukewarm Qarmathians.

Tustar: In Khuzestan, 60 miles north of Al-Ahwaz. A sectarian nexus.

Al-Ahwaz: Capital city of a fertile region watered by the River Dujayl.

The Sawad: Rich farmland but dependent on irrigation systems.

Nishapur: Home of the Chess Board Mosque.

Baghdad: The Eternal City, a lesson in mutability.

"The Baghdadi pays more for a meal than a Sawadi tax farmer pays for his wives; and the meal tastes better than the wives."

The poet Jami' screeds of a desert Bedouin overwhelmed by the Megalopolis who, before he takes a nap in Soap Boiler's Alley, ties a brick of soap around his ankle so that he can distinguish himself from a million interchangeable Baghdadis. The poem ends when Bedouin and soap are digested by the befuddled Alley. A case of mistaken identity?

Central Baghdad: Or the Round City of Mansur. In this era a Caliphal trash museum.

Mosque of Mansur: The Great Friday Mosque, gleaming with lapis lazuli tiles. Discovered like some lost landfill city every Friday by thousands of intrepid believers and by the Caliph once a year.

Western Baghdad: The Crooked.

Palace of Mu'nis: Like the Caliphal and Vizierial palaces, only reachable by canal boats.

Karkh: A commercial suburb south of the Round City.

The Pilgrim's Road: Runs southwest to Meccah.

The Clappers Guild

The House of Musical Women

Cemetery of Martyrs: Notable for its scandalous tolerance towards heretic corpses.

'Isa Canal: Feeds Western Baghdad and the suburbs before losing itself in the Tigris. Southern boundary line between the Katrabbul and Baduraya Districts. Cargo boats from Euphrates dock at the lower harbor in Karkh.

Sarat Canal: This branch of the 'Isa Canal splits north and south around the Round City.

Karkhaya Canal: A canal which splits into four kanaats, or sub-canals, feeding Karkh.

The Dog Canal: Connects Karkhaya to its parent canal, the 'Isa Canal.

Kanaat: Riches or ruin flow with or against the kanaats, in that way beloved of mass transit fanatics.

Sharawi Gate Keepers

Firdaws Al-Hukma: The Garden of Wisdom.

Soap Boiler's Alley

FIEF OF THE DOGS: Caliphal joke, referring to the wild dogs infesting Baghdad.

POULTRYER'S CANAL

THE OLD BIMARISTAN: The hospital where Ar-Razi established a medical school.

MARKET OF THE THORN SELLERS: The thorns are used for kindling ovens and heating the public bathwater.

EAST BAGHDAD: The New City. The seat of Caliphal power.

RUSAFAH: A palace which has devoured a mosque.

MUQTADIR'S PALACE: A Basilidean constellation of cages.

ASKAR AL-MAHDI: The Caliph Al-Mahdi's PIT for pickling extra princes.

THE INDECISIVE HOUSE OR THE HOUSE OF INDECISION?

DIWANS (BUREAUS)

In that distant era, the Scribal Caliphate and Mandarin-Middle-Manager China will appear in textbooks under the same name. Their histories amount to a synopsis of whatever paperwork their bureaucrats bothered to process.

Diwan of Confiscated Property

Diwan of the Sawad: Administers Southern Iraq, especially the arable regions around Basra, Kufa, Wasit, Samarra and Anbar. Next to the Bureau of Ahwaz, the most important of the diwans.

Diwan of Ahwaz: Administers the fertile swathe around the city of Al-Ahwaz, center of a great export trade to Basrah and a large warehousing district. Headquarters of the Zanj World-Breakers during their uprising.

Diwan of Intestinal Complaints: A bureau for bureaucrats to register complaints against other bureaucrats.

Diwan of Historical Astrology: With laudable courage they forecast the past.

Diwan of Strategic Miracles

Diwan of Interdiwan Cartography: Supplies office maps at a scale of 1 inch per 20 miles.

The Donation Diwan: Handles the monthly bribe paid to the Turkish slave soldiers.

APOTHEGMS

"The rose has fled the garden; what shall I do with its thorns? The bird has flown; what shall I do with the cage?"

"In praising honey, you may say. 'This is the saliva of the bee,' meaning that sweet truths appear at first repulsively."

"The treasure's gone; the dragon remains." I.E. your wife has died, saddling you with her mother-in-law.

According to Philip Hitti, the polite Christian response on refusing conversion is "I prefer the company of my fathers in hell."

Al Khwarizimi's snide remark: "The grave is the best son-in-law."

"Cracks in a wall foretell collapse; a wet wind is a sign of rain."

THE BOOK OF ROADS AND RUINED CITIES

Or 'The Book of Hallucinated Roads and Ruins' according to Bar Huthayl's hostile translation. We highlight the following passages as deserving of further study.

"In the ravaged city of Gurjan the traveler occasionally comes across holograms weeping over holograms and mud mothers cradling baby dust."

" In Outremer the Damned, City of Silence, Bar Khadim the Smuggler is snapping the necks of twelve invaluable songbirds. He's ruined; his clients are vengeful; but the Trimmers are oozing towards them, a muffled Mouthminder Mass, voracious. The brazen hotel keepers' children are waving the rufters (bird muting hoods) they've stolen like battle flags, their celebratory cawing putrefacting the birdsong still paving the wind like roadkill. Before the Mass can pass sentence, the parents suffocate their children. The Mass, having ratified the distraught vigilantes, evaporates as quietly as it jelled."

"The tupperware people never rust. They've converted this factory fortress of the forgotten frontier jihad into a typical plagueland hamlet, with dahlias tarnishing and corroding dogs, pit bulls whose pedigree is their verdigris and uterine rust. My friend for the evening, and several evenings more, takes a drag, savors her bubbling polyethylene lungs and tries to laugh. "The environment refused to change so we changed the environmentalists."

"The hostile algorithms of Saksiwa, their computational checks and balances, that Socratic stasis so long desired, abhorred."

THE RECURSION PROBLEM

The Gospel of Phillip says that Jesus was crucified on a cross made from trees he had planted for his carpentry business.

FLUTTERING FOREPLAY EFFECT

They weren't making love but destroying time. Both would have preferred blessed brain damage to post-coital bliss, and who could blame them when foreplay becomes a mass extinction event? Love is hard enough without having to worry that apologetic orgasms might exterminate sabre-tooth butterflies or some such shit effect.

CODON (EXPRESSED OR SUPPRESSED)

BATIN: The hidden self; the unbinding of human helices to reveal a "molecular text" superseding all the scriptures of the visible world.

SUBEDAR: Military rank in three grades—descendant, ascendant, superior.

ISNAAD: The chain of witnesses, whether concrete or convenient, convened to stifle controversy.

SEERA: Hagiographies of the Prophet. Often retrofitted, to justify latter-day mutations of Islam.

ILHAM: Sight of the unseen; first order revelation. According to the Sufis, the inspirational insanity of saints which they refer to as "reskinning the skinless panther."

MIHNA: The Mu'atazila inquisition against those who believe the Quran was not created but is preeternal with God.

Ulema: Hoods are worn by jurists and doctors of the law; a green hood marks superior merit.

Donative: The monthly military bribe; a major cause of the tax squeeze which ruins the Caliphate.

Haal: The frenzy wherein the Sufi initiate-mureed reunifies temporarily with God.

Ilm Al-Jafr: The science of number-letter prognostication. It is averred that the Messiah will have total mastery over this science.

Ramuz: The hermeneutic decipher-diagrams, anatomical runes and alchemical recipes used to achieve gnosis.

Irami: Earthly denizen of paradise.

Khaak: Words that molder to dust; a warning against literary arrogance.

Ghulam: Originally a beardless boy or household slave. Later used to describe Turkish slave-soldiers, the backbone of the Abbasid armies and valued for their discipline and indifference to sectarian strife.

Madhhab: Juridical rite. The more comprehensive the hadith, the less room for reasoning; to codify is to petrify.

MUTAKALLIMUN: Speculative theologians; see also Ahl Al-Kalaam, The People of the Word.

KALAAM: Islamic scholastic theology.

AL-ATHRAM: Laqab meaning The Broken Toothed One.

MOTHER OF CHILDREN: Euphemism for concubine.

FITNA: Strife; affliction.

HADITH OF THE FLAGS: A fabricated hadith, transmitted by the traditionist Ibn Abi Ziyad of Kufa which tells of black flags and a Mahdi from the East, leveraged in service of Abbasid claims to the Caliphate.

RIBAT: A militant-missionary outpost serving the frontier jihad.

ABDAL(PL.): Substitute saints damned for love, sacrificial victims.

RA'WI: Echoer-Adepts; the disciple chosen to echo or polymerize the words of the Master. The Master's posthumous voice.

WAQF: Endowment; charitable donation of land or a building.

Rafidi: The Rejectors. Insulting term used by the orthodox Consenters to refer to those who reject the first three Caliphs.

Qarmathian Dust Writing: A precarious script used by Qarmathian archivists who would rather annihilate entire libraries with a single puff than let them fall into the hands of orthodox inquisitors.

Qummi Glyph: Used by Qarmathians to encode the afterimage of cell cadres, high-value adversaries, assassination targets, and infesting maphrians.

REFERENCE BOOKS

The Preeminence of Dogs Over Clothes Wearers. Street name == *The Book of Insults*.

Kitab Al-Maw'udaat. The Fihrist refers to a historical work entitled 'Girls Buried Alive' by Hisham Al-Kalbi about the pre-Islamic method of infanticide. "It was rumored that the Banu ▓▓▓▓ still buried infant girls alive, a practice described in the Kitab Al-Maw'udaat of Ibn Al-Kalbi and formerly abolished by the Prophet."

Kitab Al-Irshad. The Lives of Ali and his successor Imams. "Then I struck him with another blow, brought him down and plundered him. I saw he had a robe of saffron and I realized he had recently been married."

Ibid. "Have you put the shroud on the Apostle of God while he is still alive? Indeed you are like the mistresses of Joseph."

Kitab Al-Jafr. The Book of Numerical Destinies. The book foreshadows (or is made to foreshadow) the Abbasid victory.

Asrar Al-Batiniya. Al-Baqalani's book on the Qarmathians. "It was the Qarmathian alchemists who invented the pill bottle (capsule) biography, digestible working class nobodies of the Jointed Brotherhood, unadulterated by heroism or infamy, but chonk full of bugminder banalities."

The Caliphal Clown Abu'l Anbas Al-Saymari, *Rare Anecdotes about Pimps and Procuresses.*

The Caliphal Clown Abu'l Anbas Al-Saymari, *The Superiority of the Rectum over the Mouth.*

The Caliphal Clown Abu'l Anbas Al-Saymari, *Refutation of the Perfumed.*

The Crawling Book. An insect book by Jahm Ibn Kahlaf Al-Mazini.

CLOAK

Learn more at https://cloak.wtf